TAKING
Liberties

MINA VAUGHN
LINDA CUNNINGHAM
JOY FULCHER
KC HOLLY
KIMBERLY JENSEN & SCOTT STARK
VIVIAN RIDER

FORWARD BY TIFFANY REISZ

OMNIFIC PUBLISHING
LOS ANGELES

Omnific Publishing
1901 Avenue of the Stars, 2nd floor
Los Angeles, CA 90067
www.omnificpublishing.com

First Omnific eBook edition, July 2014
First Omnific trade paperback edition, July 2014

Library of Congress Cataloguing-in-Publication Data

Vaughn, Mina; Cunningham, Linda; Fulcher, Joy; Holly, KC; Jensen,
Kimberly; Stark, Scott; Rider, Vivian; Reisz, Tiffany.
Taking Liberties / Mina Vaughn, Linda Cunningham, Joy Fulcher, KC Holly,
Kimberly Jensen & Scott Stark, Vivian Rider, Tiffany Reisz – 1st ed.
ISBN: 978-1-623421-68-7
1. Historical Romance — Fiction. 2. Romance — Fiction.
3. Erotica — Fiction. 4. Colonial America — Fiction. I. Title

10 9 8 7 6 5 4 3 2 1

Cover Design by Micha Stone and Amy Brokaw
Interior Book Design by Coreen Montagna

Printed in the United States of America

FORWARD

My favorite television show in middle school was a British import called *Blackadder*. Starring Rowan Atkinson as the titular character, *Blackadder* took dry English history and make a farce of it. I've always wanted a US version of *Blackadder* that made a mockery of our country's own checkered history. And now we have it!

Taking Liberties began as a tweet. One of my tweets. My tweets have been responsible for more ridiculous ideas than I'm comfortable confessing to. I joked on Twitter that someday I would write an erotic retelling of the American Revolution and call it *Pounding Fathers*. My friends at Omnific (crazy wenches that they are) actually thought this was a good idea.

So here it is, my dream come true. A rollicking, rolling, heaving, happy, sexy, and wild re-imagining of our Founding Fathers and what they might have done with their mighty quills when they weren't busy signing the Declaration of Independence.

Writers of *Taking Liberties*, I salute you. America was founded on the principle of free speech—and if an anthology making sexy mockery of our Founding Fathers isn't the very heart of free speech, then I don't know what is.

Although, I still think my title was better.

Historically Yours,
Tiffany Reisz
Accidental Founding Mother of *Taking Liberties*

JOHN HANCOCK-BLOCKED

BY MINA VAUGHN

John Hancock

John Hancock

John Hancock

Over and over, I had signed my name on the practice parchment my uncle had given me. As the man who would inherit Hancock House, and one of the wealthiest young men in the colonies, I knew I'd have to acquire an impressive signature that would be worthy of my future stature.

But I certainly couldn't do that with a quill that needed re-nubbing.

And frankly, I could use a bit of nubbing myself, if you follow. The ladies in Quincy were quite prudish, wanting to impress wealthy young lads like me by being paragons of virtue instead of showing a little flesh once in a while when out by the stables.

Bah.

I left Hancock House and strolled down to the local printer and binder's store. I'd oft stop there to send a parcel or to deliver some news to like-minded patriots, but today I just wanted a quill and an eyeful of Hazel Marron. Ah, Hazel. Her bosoms floated up to her throat as though her chin needed a place to rest.

I would rest more than my chin there.

Hazel had always fascinated me. Her appearance was certainly worthy of attention—round green eyes, full lips, and a curvy body—but it was her behavior that had me positively stumped. She stood and spoke at local meetings the way a man would. She looked me in the eye and did not blush or stutter. Hazel Marron was as clever and bold as any man I had ever met.

This intrigued me as much as it inflamed my loins.

Pushing my way into the store, I sagged with disappointment at the absence of the brazen beauty. Hazel's father was behind the counter, not the lovely lass herself. However, there was a new batch of fine quills available, which was ostensibly the reason for my visit. These ones were from special geese, bred for their long and stiff feathers.

And once Hazel stepped out from the back room, my own "feather" followed suit. She stood with erect posture, and I marveled at the bold way she displayed her prodigious breasts. Most girls would humbly cover them. Not Hazel. She was, dare I say, proud of her sinful body.

"I must get to the smithy," her father said in an anxious voice, handing her a parcel, "so please tend to the store in my absence."

Hazel nodded—well, as much as her cleavage would allow without her face bumping into her breasts—and he left.

I glanced around the store. We were alone! How would I approach her? All of the young men in town were so intimidated by her that she rarely was seen around town with anyone. I knew my name made me quite the catch, but I didn't know if I could even summon the courage to speak to her.

"Hello, Mister Hancock," she purred, leaning over the counter at my arrival. She virtually spilt her wares out of her dress! I blinked several times before responding, trying to burn the lovely image into my brain. A thrill of joy shot through my body at the fact that she not only knew me, but was clearly glad to see me.

"Hello, Miss Marron," I said, striding up to the desk with confidence. My eyes boldly followed the curves of her chest, then finally up to her eyes, which were gleaming at me.

"What can I do for you today, good sir?"

I stiffened. In many ways. "Err…I'd like a few good, hard, long quills." I nearly fainted at my wording. It was like my cock took control of my mouth and…*suggested things* to her. Salacious things!

"Mmmm," she said, rolling her eyes back. "I think I can help." She licked her lips and winked.

I nearly swallowed my tongue. Was she…flirting with me? The lick and wink were clearly sexual. Perhaps she would respond to more sensual imagery?

My eyes dipped back to her bosom, which was blooming with a pink blush. "Yes, I'd like a nice bottle of ink as well. Something deep for me to really sink my quill into." Much bolder language than I'd normally use, but she was sending me signals with her eyes and her mouth. Oh good, I may just get that re-nubbing!

Hazel straightened, pushed her chest out, and fanned herself. "My, it's warm for March," she said, and loosened the top of her corset. I watched her breasts jiggle out of their tight constraints and nearly "spilled my ink."

"Do you have something that would suit my quill?" I asked, tempted to unlace my trousers in the same manner. I glanced back at the door — nobody was in sight. I wondered how long her father would be out.

Hazel's long, chestnut curls were pinned back into a conservative bun whenever she worked, but I watched her arms move up toward her hair. Her fingers fiddled, and soon a cascade of ringlets fell around her shoulders, framing her gorgeous décolletage. "Yes, I do," she whispered, licking her lips again. She should get some balm for that. "Would you like to come behind the counter?"

At the words "come" and "behind," my feet just about hopped into the air. Finally, a girl who wasn't afraid to get a little friendly with a gentleman like me! More importantly, it was the bold and brazen girl I couldn't get out of my head.

Just then, a tinkling sound rang out behind me and a customer came in.

I deflated like a weak sail and Hazel tucked her curls behind her ears demurely.

Confound it!

Old Ben waddled in, packages stacked up to his round spectacles. "Good afternoon," he warbled, slowly ambling his way to the counter, paying no mind to the two worked-up young folks who were clearly breathless and irritated at his entrance.

"Hello," she said sadly, and began processing his packages. I leaned against the counter, away from Ben, trying to hide my predicament.

"Is that you, young Hancock?" he asked.

I nodded. "Good day, sir."

"How are things at old Hancock House?"

My mouth wanted to frown, but I couldn't offend the statesman. "Business as usual."

He laughed and slapped my shoulder hard. "Tell your uncle I said hello."

I nodded and he finished paying.

The moment he was out the door, I turned toward Hazel—

—who was slowly unlacing the rest of her corset. The top of her blouse was thin enough for me to see through, once the tight boning set her breasts free, and I was able to make out her round and luscious bosoms. She was leaning forward, mere inches from my face.

I took her chin in my hand and kissed her softly. She opened her lips and slipped her tongue inside my mouth. My hands were still by my sides, and I wondered what a bold girl like Hazel would want me to do. Her tongue flicked at mine, caressing my lips, and I tried to meet her strokes with my own. She hummed into my mouth, and the sound went straight to my cock. Her hands unlaced her shirt more and I peeked open my eyes and saw heaven. I reached across the counter and slipped my hand inside her shirt, palming that silky flesh and giving her a squeeze. My entire hand couldn't fit around her ample tit, and so I began to reach my other arm across to take off her top entirely and feel her body beneath my grasp—

—when the door tinkled again.

Hazel ducked behind the counter and I was left there, hands open for breasts that were gone. I tucked my lonely fingers into my coat pocket and pulled the jacket outward as to hide my enthusiasm for Hazel's fine form.

Another customer entered, this time an older woman with a severe gray bun and a withered, sour face.

"Where is Mister Marron?" she asked me.

"Pardon me, but I'm afraid he is out at the smithy. Would you be able to return in an hour?" I asked, buying time. Not that I'd need more than probably ten minutes, but I had to assure that Hazel and I would have enough time for us to enjoy each other's company, if you follow.

Her hard, joyless mouth drooped further down. "I suppose," she replied and swiftly left, her wrinkled bustle swaying as she exited the door.

"Is there a lock?" I asked, fumbling to find a way to keep people out.

Hazel popped up from beneath the counter, hair a gorgeous mess and tits virtually falling out of her see-through top. "Up by the top of the door is a hook and eye."

"Aye," I groaned, fidgeting with the latch until it was thoroughly locked.

She stood there, smirking, twirling a lock of brown hair. "Are you coming?" she said coyly.

"Not yet," I replied with a wink and dashed toward her. I vaulted over the counter, recalling my days as a spry young athlete, and landed right in front of her. I traced my finger across the soft skin of her chest, spelling my name. "Now there is some paper I'd like to scrawl my ink across."

Her neck arched back in rapture. "Mark me, John Hancock."

"I shall practice first with my tongue," I said, pulling the linen blouse from her shoulders, freeing her breasts. I cupped them in my hands, rubbing her pink nipples with my thumbs, and began to lick my signature across her chest.

I began with the J right under her arm, just beginning to lick the side of her bosom. She moaned, and I watched her nipples tighten and harden. I couldn't wait to get to H or N. My O slid across the heavy swell of skin and I marveled at how soft and silky she tasted against my tongue. Desperation built inside me and I wanted to remove my trousers and be quick about my satisfaction, but there was something about marking her with my name that felt so necessary. The H slid across her nipple, and I decided to take a moment from my writing lessons to suckle a bit. She moaned as I took her nipple into my mouth, and she grabbed my hair, pushing me further toward her. My right hand caressed her left breast, and I continued my wet slide across her heaving tits.

"Hazel!" someone cried, knocking frantically. "Why is the door locked? Hazel, I forgot the horseshoes! Open up!"

I skittered back and looked into Hazel's wide eyes. "Father," she mouthed, pulling her top back up and lacing it quickly. "Stay behind here!" she said in a worried whisper.

"I shut down the shop because I was worried I couldn't handle customers without you!" she shouted at the locked door. "Do you need me to fetch you the horseshoes?"

The knocking ceased. "Yes, yes," he muttered, annoyed. Hazel dashed into the back room and quickly returned, holding several well-worn horseshoes.

She opened the door a crack and looked at her father disapprovingly. "Really, father, next time you head to the smithy, please do make sure you have what needs fixing."

He chuckled, took the shoes from her, and left without another word.

Hazel locked the door and eyed me with a fiery expression.

"Get your quill back here," she said, crooking her finger at me. "I've got your deep well ready."

I bit my lip. "Is it dripping?"

She nodded. "I hope you plan to write a lot, because I want that quill in and out of my bottle for a very long time."

This time I undid my trousers before leaping over the counter. My breeches fell to the ground after my vault, but I didn't care.

"My, my, I see now why your signature is so…large and impressive," she said, glancing down.

"That's because I practice," I said, pulling her toward me. I felt her hand wrap around me and I shuddered. Her bravery was making me even bolder than I had imagined. "I like to swirl my quill around in the ink, pull it out, and just scrawl my signature as many times as I can."

She moaned.

"And then I plunge it back in and do it again."

"Put your John Hancock in me," she moaned, fussing with her skirts.

I helped her, trying to push away all the frippery and get right down to her knickers. I wondered why women's undergarments were so fluffy and unnecessary. I wanted to feel the skin of her thighs beneath my hands, but all I could manage was folds of lace and linen.

Decidedly not the folds I was hoping to finger, if you follow.

"Quickly," she breathed, leaning back against the counter. "I cannot wait any longer."

I fumbled around in the mess of fabric and decided this was possibly worse than someone ringing at the door. Here she was, delicious and waiting for me, and I couldn't get past her absurd skirts!

"Here," she said, finally getting to the bottom of her petticoats and pulling down the last layer.

I wanted to shout for joy.

Hazel pushed her legs open. "I'd like another signature before that quill, if you have time," she said, giggling.

Running my hands up her thighs, I decided I wouldn't mind at all. "But of course," I said, spreading her sex and tracing J with my tongue. I knew that this was something men often did, and typically it was so that the act would be reciprocated. But I didn't care for that at the moment...all I wanted was to please this wild, carefree woman. I was positively enraptured with her.

"Oh, God! I wish you had a longer name!" She moaned as I licked each letter into her hot, wet body. My hands grasped her hips as she bucked against my tongue, frantic and desperate for release. For the final O in my last name, right before the CK, I decided to go slowly. I traced the O in small circles around her clit until she finally trembled, and I finished her up with a neat C and K as she leaned, trembling, against the counter.

Just then, shouts sounded in the street.

Our eyes met and hers widened in fear.

I stood and put my hand on her shoulder as I listened. A woman screamed and Hazel gasped.

Part of me wanted to stay here and forget what was going on outside. I'm sure anyone could guess what that part was.

But the patriot in me, the proud man of House Hancock, had to make sure things in my fine colony of Massachusetts were going well. Tensions with the British had begun to get very heated, and just last week the damned bastards had commandeered my boat and locked it up for smuggling. Me! A smuggler?

I had to see what this was about.

Arranging myself as best I could, I unlocked the door and poked my head out. A British soldier was harassing a young woman.

"Take her to the governor," one said, poking his musket at her with a snarl.

"What is going on here?" I asked, stepping forward.

A soldier nodded. "Ah, Mister Hancock. This woman has been accused of stealing from the Adams' stable down the road. Took some tack, from what I hear."

The woman trembled and shook her head. "Lies!"

I stepped forward. "Unhand her."

The soldiers did not stand down, but one lowered his weapon and listened.

"This woman is employed by my estate. Let me handle her judgment."

She widened her eyes, but as I glanced at her, understanding settled upon her face. She knew I was trying to help.

The eldest soldier shook his head. "This isn't your business, Hancock."

I stepped forward, emboldened by my encounter with Hazel and also my anxiousness to get back to her. "My servants are my business; now unhand her and let my uncle deal with this accusation. You know we and the Adamses are practically kin. We will take care of it."

The soldier frowned and waved us on. "As you were," he said, and they ran off.

The woman looked at me with kind, red-rimmed eyes. "Thank you."

"Did you take it?" I asked softly, non-accusingly.

She shook her head. "That soldier tried to have his way with me. I wouldn't let him. Then he told his compatriots that false story and tried to arrest me."

I frowned. "I shall take you home myself," I said, disappointed I'd have to be away from Hazel, but sure in my duty as a protector of this colony.

She shook her head. "My brother's right in the bakery. He can walk me home."

Relief spread through my body. "Ah, good. Best wishes," I said and saluted her.

As though my fingers were on fire, I unlocked the door to the Marron's shop and re-entered—

—to find Hazel's naked and curvaceous form sprawled across the high countertop, her leg dangling. "So glad you've come back."

Again I blinked, letting the image settle into every corner of my brain. She was so gorgeous, with her round green eyes and her long, shapely legs. My body recalled its previous state of arousal and I approached the counter with a hunger like I'd never before felt.

"How long will your father be at the smithy?" I asked, running my finger along the curve of her hips.

"No less than an hour," she said, quirking an eyebrow at me. "Long enough to get these off." She slipped her hand inside my trousers and grasped my cock. "And long enough for you to practice your penmanship with this big quill here."

It was all the prompting I needed.

I removed all my clothing, so I could be as naked and beautiful Hazel was, and mounted the high countertop. Her legs were spread beneath me and they fell to either side, dangling toward the ground. It felt riskier this way, more dangerous. We weren't hiding our arousal beneath clothes, we weren't tucked away behind a counter. We were naked, on display in front of the whole store, and we were about to join.

Positioning myself between Hazel's legs, I placed my hands over her breasts and slid inside her with one deep push. I felt her tense beneath me, then relax as I pulsed in and out. I was amazed at how soft her body could feel, and yet how strongly her legs clenched around me. Thrusting harder, I pulled her hips up and worked her body with a new angle. She screamed, and I had to put my hand over her mouth as a caution. She licked my palm, and I slid my hand from her mouth and laced it into her hair as I rode her harder. Hazel was feisty and thrust her hips back at me in retaliation, as though she were the one in charge. I felt a tingle at that thought, and decided that although it was deemed unmanly, I wanted her on top.

I pulled out and sat up on the counter. Hazel frowned, but I guided her legs as to suggest the new position without saying so. I was...embarrassed to want her on top.

She smiled, though, and took the tacit control that I had handed her. She positioned me between her legs and slammed down on me. I gripped the counter, worried I'd fall off. She was so...aggressive! Her bosoms, which she had hidden from me earlier behind the wall of satin and linen, were now bouncing and free and jiggling in my face. I couldn't help myself, so I took one into my mouth and sucked heartily. Hazel approved with a moan and rode me with even more abandon. What a liberated woman!

I wanted to reward her for the enthusiasm she displayed. All the other women I had been with were so quiet and reserved during sex, as though they were afraid of it. But Hazel, she was destined for pleasure. Her eyes, alight with passion. Her mouth, wet and swollen from kisses. And, oh my, those bouncing bosoms. Each and every part of her was made for the act of love. I placed my hands between us and rubbed her clit, wanting so badly for her to come again. I had never felt such an urge to please a woman, but the way she felt earlier when I had used my tongue on her was reward enough. I was happy to see that my manipulations worked quickly, as she cried my name and collapsed forward onto my chest.

I ran my fingers through her hair as she breathed hard against my skin, rocking only gently now. I chuckled; she was exhausted. I placed a kiss on her mouth and re-positioned her back down on the counter.

She shook her head, no.

"I want you from behind," she purred, hopping down onto the ground and pulling a blanket out from beneath the counter. She held it up. "I usually use this when I'm cold, not when I'm…hot." She giggled, and folded it neatly under her hands and knees.

I swallowed hard as she wiggled her ass at me. A liberated woman indeed.

Kneeling along with her, I caressed her roundness before penetrating her again. Her buttocks were just as soft and curvy as her breasts, and I gave them a light slap on each side as she giggled.

"Now, make sure you practice that name of yours," she said with another wiggle. "You just pull out of the bottle and sprawl your ink."

At her bold suggestion, I couldn't hold back any more, and pushed inside her again. She moaned hard, clearly pleased with the new angle. I placed my hands on her hips and thrust into her, watching her body respond to mine so beautifully.

"Harder, John Hancock," she grunted.

Harder? Usually women wanted it slower, gentler.

"R-Really?" I stuttered.

She pushed back with a buck.

Ah, I see.

I gripped her hips harder and gave a mighty moan as I thrust quickly and thoroughly. Squeals of approval rang from her round lips, and again and again I pushed so deeply inside her, I couldn't go a fraction further. I slid one hand from her hip up her body to her breast and rubbed her nipple.

Within seconds, she was coming again. The stamina of this woman! I wondered if I shouldn't buy more than one quill so I could come back here once a week for more visits with Hazel. She was so unique in her sexuality; I couldn't get enough of her.

But, of course, after a few more minutes of her moans and her curves and her hard nipple under my thumb, it was time to practice my name once more.

"Give me that John Hancock," she cried as I pulled out and spelled my name one last time on the skin of her back.

Moments later, we were dressed and chatting casually, as though we hadn't spent the last hour aroused and pleasuring one another. She sold me a pen and gave me a complimentary sheet of the whitest paper I had ever seen.

"It's so smooth," I said, admiring.

She winked. "I hope you'll practice on it and think of me. And maybe come back for another sheet sometime soon."

I smiled, glad she wanted the same thing. More little trysts together. "If I could make signing my name my job, I would."

Hazel giggled. "Promise me you'll think of me each time you write it. Make it long, curvy, and impossible to ignore."

I reached out and shook her hand. "It's a deal."

She tapped her chest. "Then sign."

My eyes widened. "But your father will be back soon!"

Hazel shrugged. "I have a cloak that will cover it."

I picked up my new quill and dipped it in ink as she opened her blouse again.

And right across her glorious chest, I put my John Hancock.

THE BRITISH ARE COMING!

BY KC HOLLY

During the Revolutionary War, the British regularly quartered their troops in private homes, a practice our Founding Fathers felt was objectionable enough to specifically restrict in the Third Amendment to the US Constitution. Is it possible those Founding Fathers were a bit too hasty, a little too worried about what those quartered troops were up to while they were away? I mean, who doesn't love a man in uniform...

Col. Lord Edward Swinton
British Army, Philadelphia, 1777

I fully expected to be bored beyond measure while quartered in this cultural wasteland. Admittedly, it was one of the more elegant homes in Philadelphia, with cultivated grounds and pristine stabling for my horses. But dear God, the occupants. I suppose I should have been content to be housed with such devoted loyalists, but their obsequiousness was tedious in the extreme, forcing me to avoid them whenever possible. Indeed, the only feature of any interest was an extremely fetching maidservant of some kind, perhaps a kitchen maid or one who tended the domesticated animals, for I never caught sight of her in the house proper.

I rarely got to experience the thrill of the hunt. If it wasn't my looks or money, usually the title and estates brought women running. But this promised to be different. Even from a distance the girl intrigued me, casting a bold gaze while adopting an otherwise timid manner. I was anxious to learn more.

I spotted her from the window of my bedchamber one morning, and when she espied me, she stared back for a moment before sauntering off to her work. Did I notice a bit of a saucy lilt to her walk? It soon became a morning habit to look for her, and I began to detect an air of self-satisfaction in the occasional smile she gave me. I looked for her whenever the occasion led me from the house, and began to collect my own horse at the stable yard, hoping for a closer glimpse, with which I was soon rewarded.

She had a sweet, heart-shaped face framed by dark hair, a few errant tendrils provocatively escaping her demure, white mob cap. An innocent, I concluded. Yet the kerchief designed to protect her modesty often seemed carelessly affixed, and rather than covering her charms, its placement seemed to focus all attention on what were undoubtedly her two most prominent attractions. No innocent then, she. And my internal debate continued in this way, until I burned to discover the truth for myself. Was she slattern or saint? I hoped for a bit of both.

My opportunity arose when returning from a morning ride. Coming into the stable yard, I noticed her entering the stables. Without further thought, I dismounted and flung the reins to a groom. Tossing him a fat coin, I turned back to him before shutting the stable door.

"This door shall remain closed until I emerge," I instructed the groom. With a sly smile, he led my horse away.

As my eyes adjusted to the shadows of the stable, I glanced around, looking for my prize. Apparently she had just finished milking the family cows before letting them out to pasture, as she was struggling a bit to adjust a yolk across her shoulders to carry the pails of milk into the house.

She looked perfect. On her head, she wore the usual mob cap with her hair tucked inside, leaving her graceful neck open to my view. On her feet were black, buckled shoes, and I could see a bit of her white stockings peeking from just below the hem of her blue skirt. It was teased up a bit on one side, so the ruffles of the bright white petticoat underneath peeked out. Over a white shift, her black bodice was tight and laced up the front, and what it did for her glorious bosom was breathtaking. With the neckline scooping low on her breasts, some degree of support was afforded, but the garment did little to contain them. The globes of delectable flesh were exquisitely positioned, protruding outward and yet pushed together at the same time. They looked…*edible*. Her usual kerchief was simply draped across her neck, obscuring nothing. She adjusted the yolk on the back of her neck to her liking and with ease lifted the pails of milk.

She was the exact picture of the fetching milkmaid, somehow managing to look virtuous but naughty, all at the same time. My already animated cock fully hardened, a fact that could hardly go unnoticed in my tight breeches.

"Well, well, well, what have we here?" I asked while lashing my riding crop lightly against my leg, slowly approaching her.

"Good day, my Lord," the girl answered with a tremulous smile. She gave me a brazen look before dropping her gaze to the ground, as if remembering to appear modest.

"And you are?" I prompted, beginning to circle around her like a shark eyeing its helpless prey.

"I'm Betsy, my Lord, the milkmaid," she answered shyly. Or was it coyness?

I stopped in front of her, edging closer until I was about a foot away. Removing my hat, I threw it on a bale of hay. I lifted the riding crop and dragged the end across the top of her breasts. "And tell me, Betsy, are you a good milkmaid?"

"M-My Lord, p-please," she stuttered. "I'll spill the milk!"

"No, Betsy. You shan't spill the milk. You would not want me to inform my hosts of the careless servant they have. If you spill even a drop of that milk, I will do so. Do you understand?" I tried to look quite stern, forced to bite on the inside of my cheeks to avoid an ear-splitting evil grin.

"Yes, my Lord," she said obediently, pouting fetchingly.

"Now, Betsy…" I began in a low, husky voice, "I want you to teach me something, and remember—" I gestured to the pails with my crop " —you mustn't spill a drop."

"T-Teach you, my Lord? What could *I* teach *you?*"

"All about…milking, my sweet." I used my riding crop to gently poke the tip of her breast. "You look singularly qualified to instruct me…"

Betsy's eyes went wide, and my cock got even harder. It was going to stab a hole through these fucking breeches if this kept up.

I threw the crop aside and raised my hands to her top. Untying the drawstring, I peeled the soft fabric down, exposing much of her breasts. And they looked just as tantalizing as I thought they would, supported just enough to extend forward, their fullness plumped together and *oh, my*...I unintentionally licked my lips.

Betsy assumed an expression of utmost distress, one I found most insincere. She looked up at me, eyes wide and pleading, and said, "Oh, my Lord..." I noticed she didn't object or collapse into maidenly tears.

My cock responded to her pleas. "But I need you to teach me, and with a lovely, full pair of teats like this, you must be...especially talented," I purred evilly. I shifted her bodice down further, and enclosing a breast in each hand, I began to roughly grope them, squeezing rhythmically. "Is this the way?"

Betsy closed her eyes, as if ashamed—*fucking perfect!*—while I continued my rough, awkward caresses.

"Perhaps this isn't quite the technique for milking," I said in a guttural whisper. "Maybe this would work better..." And I moved my attention to her nipples, giving them a sharp pinch, which elicited the sweetest whimper from Betsy. As I continued to twist and roll her nipples between my fingers, her lips parted and her breath came faster. This had the effect of making her chest rise and fall rapidly, such that I could simply apply pressure to her nipples and her own panting was creating the tension that was now making her moan.

"Remember, Betsy, don't spill a drop," I reminded her in a harsh whisper as I lowered my head to her chest. One hand squeezed one of her breasts, plumping the nipple up, and I clamped my mouth around it. Suckling forcefully, my free hand engaged her other nipple, manipulating it enthusiastically. I switched breasts every so often, but continued until I thought my back would give out. I did love it when nipples got tender, making them *so* sensitive to the slightest touch.

Betsy was breathing hard and moaning "Oh, my Lord" now and again, which I found motivating beyond thought. Other than that, she was remaining admirably still, and I don't think she had spilled any milk at all. Well, she was going to be punished in any event.

After fully satisfying myself with my...milking, I told Betsy, "You can put the buckets down now, my sweet."

Betsy carefully lowered the pails to the ground. Then she stood there submissively, awaiting further instructions. I lowered myself to my knees, sat back on my heels, and lifted Betsy's skirts, taking a long, satisfying scan of what I found. Her white stockings were held up just above the knee by adorable pink ribbons tied in bows on the side. Then came an expanse of lovely white flesh, and as her skirt was raised to completely exhibit her lower body, even more pearly skin, the only variation being the dark curls framing her femininity. It was a breathtaking sight.

Betsy breathed, "Please...my Lord..." *or was that "please me..."* So I indulged her.

"Hold your skirt up," I demanded, shoving the handfuls of fabric upward so she could take over. "Now, spread your legs."

She hesitated before she whimpered imploringly, and when I did nothing but continue to stare at her most vulnerable spot, her feet finally began edging apart. At six inches I harshly demanded "wider," and then reiterated, "Keep your skirt up." Servants really did need to be ordered around to maintain discipline.

When about ten inches separated her feet, I looked up again. It was such a beautiful sight. Betsy's eyes were closed, shameful desire etching her features. From this angle I could clearly see her naked breasts protruding from her bodice, evidence of my recent attentions to her nipples obvious. Both of her hands held her skirt up high, seemingly in invitation. Vulnerability exuded from her every pore. How I loved making her display herself for me. My breath caught as I devoured every square inch of the scene before me.

"Oh, my Lord, what are you doing to me?" Betsy lamented, but I swore she just suppressed a giggle.

My hands extended around her thighs before grabbing both cheeks of her ass, hard. Her feet slipped even further apart and her sex lurched forward, into my face where I wanted it. My mouth latched on with the same enthusiasm I had employed on her nipples, and too soon Betsy was writhing against my face, sobbing in need. Her hands moved to either side of my head, pulling my mouth harder into her flesh, her skirt dropping over my head, enveloping me in darkness. And suddenly there was nothing but her, squirming, slippery, undulating into my mouth as I devoured her furiously. Her exquisite moans reverberated through the rafters of the stable.

Suddenly screaming, she grabbed frantically at my head, inserting her flesh even more firmly into my mouth when her body stiffened, and for a moment it seemed that my hands were the only thing holding her up. Then even that failed, and she fell to her knees, panting wildly, looking with glazed eyes around the barn as if salvation lay there. Her mob cap had been lost somewhere along the way, and her dark hair cascaded down her shoulders, as lovely as I had imagined.

Luckily, on her knees just happened to be perfect for what I had in mind next.

"Now, my sweet," I managed, desire choking my voice, "you shall suckle me." I gave her nipples another sharp pinch to make sure I had her full attention.

Betsy refocused on my face, giving me a look of adorable confusion. "My Lord?" she questioned weakly.

I stood and unbuttoned my breeches, pulling them down my legs a sufficient amount. I shoved my shirt to the side and displayed my aroused condition to her. She licked her lips and gave me a look of nervous dismay at the same time.

"Oh, my Lord," she exclaimed, her voice thick with emotion, "whatever can you mean?"

"Come now, my dear, I mean what I said. Put it in your mouth and…suckle." I thrust my cock toward her face.

She hesitated still, and *oh my God*, momentarily chewed on a fingertip in consternation as if I couldn't possibly mean what I said, although clearly, this wasn't the first erection she'd ever seen.

She continued to stall until I realized that this could be for my benefit. Whether or no it was, I decidedly took advantage of it. "Open your mouth and I shall show you," I instructed as I put a hand on each side of her head.

Tipping her face upward, I gasped sharply as I saw her obediently kneeling before me, her lovely breasts on display, her mouth open wide, her eyes closed. With as much restraint as I could muster, I inserted my cock into her mouth and demanded, "Suck."

Was it my wishful thinking, or did she seem to be ceding command to me, pushing her face forward to take me in while her hands remained idle by her sides? Whether that was the case or not, I couldn't help taking advantage, although I managed to avoid, barely, shoving my cock down her throat. I kept my gaze glued to my length as it disappeared into her mouth, and I'm positive she never showed any signs of distress, just sweetly sucking me as I moved in and out with enthusiasm, grunting with every thrust.

Sooner than I wanted, it became too much. "Oh, my God, oh, suck me hard," I suddenly exclaimed. I was lunging faster now, holding her head steady, and I could feel my balls starting to tighten. "Swallow…

it," I croaked in demand as my seed began to stream into her mouth. I held onto her head as my rhythmic outbursts become louder and louder. Thankfully, I was able to stay upright until I removed my cock from between her teeth, and then it was my turn to drop to my knees.

As soon as my breathing recovered a bit, I clamped my mouth around one of her impertinent nipples, sucking vigorously to her responding moans. Yes, that's what I wanted — to torment my little milkmaid some more.

"Beautiful..." I whispered onto her skin, desiring more, always more.

I pulled up my breeches and fastened a button, enabling me to stand and pick Betsy up in my arms to carry her into the corner where I had earlier noticed a clean pile of hay. I set her down, looking her over, pondering my next move. *Too many clothes...*

I unbuttoned her skirt and petticoat and quickly drew them down her legs, chuckling at Betsy's yelp as I stripped them off her and threw them aside. Her hands went to modestly cover her center, and I gave an impatient growl. Her eyes widened and she hesitantly withdrew her hands, slowly spreading her legs open. I found her submission most erotic.

Now the sight before me was much more entrancing, and I enjoyed it at my leisure. Staring at her now, her breasts jutting out, her thighs naked and trembling, her sex accessible at my whim, well, there was just no stopping me...

I leaned over Betsy, gave her a fleeting but intense kiss, and announced gleefully, "And now, my sweet, since you have so generously instructed me, I shall teach you how to ride." I gave her a sinful leer.

"But, my Lord, I am afraid of horses!" Betsy insisted in utter and completely disingenuous dismay.

I almost laughed out loud, adopting an indulgent smile instead. "Don't worry, my dear. Your riding does not require a horse."

I stripped off my uniform jacket and waistcoat, untied the cravat, and unbuttoned my shirt, pushing it out of the way. I always enjoyed the sense of vulnerability women displayed when they were more unclothed than I, so I left it on. Pushing my breeches back down to my knees, my cock now stood, proud and strong once again. I lay on my back, grabbing Betsy and dragging her body so that she was lying on top of mine. Her breasts looked so delectable from this position, they decided my starting point.

"First, some more...milking, I think."

Betsy moaned and began to struggle a bit then. I captured her arms and dragged her body upward, making sure her feminine flesh was aligned with my cock so I could enjoy her struggles even more. Yes, now every movement of her hips massaged my length, adding to the pleasure immensely. When her breasts were suspended above my mouth, I clamped my lips around a nipple and hummed with pleasure. I truly loved the idea of making my little maid take an active role in her own debauching, so after I had suckled one nipple to my satisfaction, I demanded, "Now the other one."

Delight filled me when Betsy made the necessary adjustments to shift her other nipple between my open lips. She lowered her shoulders sufficiently so I got a good mouthful, and soon the movement of her lower body subtly altered as desire flamed anew in her. As her hips began to increase their pace, undulating harder and faster against my cock, a need for more urgency…arose, so I stopped my torment of her nipples, taking a moment longer to fondle her breasts roughly and admire the moist pink nubs, now practically aglow from my exhaustive treatment of them.

I pushed Betsy upright until she was seated atop me, her legs naturally opening to straddle my torso. Grasping her hips, I lifted her body up, away from mine, telling her to be still when she reached the proper height. I removed both my hands, used one to position my cock, and demanded that Betsy ease herself down, letting her set the pace. Joy filled me as she slowly impaled herself on my cock, a series of delectable mewls escaping her. *God, I loved that…*

"Now ride, my sweet," I harshly demanded. "And ride hard."

I was so pleased I had removed her skirts, watching with rapt eyes as her intimate flesh met mine. She began to move cautiously, but I was indulgent, letting Betsy find her gait.

I shifted some more straw under my head, positioning myself for a comfortable, up-close view of our joining, my eyes glancing upward now and again to see her breasts springing about—a truly inspiring sight. Having apparently gotten the hang of it, or perhaps just inspired as well, Betsy began to bounce enthusiastically up and down, riding my cock harder. And I realized that if she kept this up, I wouldn't last long enough to bring her to release again, which I desperately wanted to do.

I splayed my hands on her hips and used both thumbs to simultaneously massage the flesh closest to her most sensitive spot. Betsy moaned loudly, throwing her head back and exclaiming, "Yes, my Lord, yes!"

More determined than ever, my thumbs moved faster while the growing speed of her bucking hips increased the manipulation of her inflamed flesh. Betsy's cries became harsher, louder, methodical. I could already tell this was going to be a good one, and I began to let myself grow more conscious of the relentless, tight caresses my cock was enjoying inside her. Suddenly she threw her head back, her body arched and frozen, a strangled cry escaping her throat, and if I hadn't already been at the brink, that image alone, of her tortured release, would have thrown me over the edge. I felt my own body stiffen and a series of harsh grunts accompanied the pulsing of my climax inside her.

Betsy wrenched my hands away from her sensitive flesh and collapsed atop me, shivering and clawing lightly at my chest. My hands rose naturally to stroke her back to comfort my poor, spent little milkmaid.

I realized it was going to take some time to recover from that little escapade, so my hands continued their travels, expanding their territory, extending downward to Betsy's lovely ass and thighs. A tiny whimper left her, because, of course, she knew I wasn't done with her yet. A paltry two orgasms could hardly be enough for my sweet girl. And while further…endeavors were beyond me at the moment, I had learned that the swiftest way to recover was to amuse myself with my plaything.

I turned us over and let Betsy roll onto her back, propping myself up on my side to lie next to her and gaze with admiration at her spent figure. Her hands came to rest on either side of her head, while her legs were lazily splayed outward, her whole demeanor one of surrender. *Yes!* I reveled in my latest victory. "Don't move," I whispered in her ear.

Betsy pried her eyes open and looked at me suspiciously.

Her breasts looked so tempting in this position, nipples pointing defiantly upward, the saucy little rascals. I took it easy on her at first, simply feathering my fingers over the silken skin, circling the rosy peaks, heightening her anticipation of when I might strike. Then my hand flew to her thigh, grasping her leg above the knee, bending and hitching it upward to lean against me, opening her further for my explorations. I sensed the momentary tensing of her body, when I'm sure she thought to shift her legs back together, but was immensely pleased that she relaxed again, putting herself at my mercy. *Of which I would have none…*

I lowered my mouth to one of those pert nipples, gently nibbling, while my fingers began to lightly trail up and down the inside of her thigh. I entertained myself like this for a while, teasing each tender peak, occasionally giving a sharper nip which would cause Betsy to moan and roll her head from side to side. And then my fingers on her thigh progressed further downward, finally stopping to infiltrate her tender flesh. My touch danced gently, and I lifted my head from the torment of her nipples to focus all my attention on her swollen feminine flesh.

I repositioned myself to sit between Betsy's outspread legs. My cock was now showing signs of life, starting to thrum with need. But first I wanted to witness Betsy's complete undoing, watch the desire overcome her again even while her body protested such overuse. So my fingers began their deliberate movements, while Betsy fought me with her sounds, moaning her objections while, to my utter delight, whispering "Oh, yes" from time to time.

I touched her nowhere else, singling out her most sensitive flesh for all my efforts, seeking only to bring her the ultimate pleasure. Now the tenor of her movements evolved, and Betsy began to rock her hips a bit, needing to increase the pressure of my hand and accelerate the movement of my fingers. I gazed down at her rapturously, struck by her beauty as she lay helpless in front of me, her eyes closed, her now unbound hair wild, her lovely breasts lewdly dancing with her movements, her lips parted to allow the frantic intake of air as her chest quickly rose and fell with her strained breathing, and finally, her glistening feminine flesh, so vulnerable between her widespread legs to whatever I desired. I watched, mesmerized, seeing the primitive impulses take command and her whole being become concentrated on one spot, on one goal.

When the moment struck, Betsy's shriek echoed through the stable, and moments later she jerked herself away from me, curling up on her side, her breaths coming in loud sobs. I hovered over her body on all fours, and for some reason bent down and licked the side of her face in one long stroke, Betsy responding with a shiver. I nuzzled her ear while her breathing slowed, and when it seemed she had recovered—well, as much as she was going to—I made my intentions clear.

"Since we're in a stable, it seems only fitting we behave like animals," I announced in a guttural whisper. I ignored her moan of denial as I snaked an arm around her middle and lifted her bodily onto her hands and knees.

Keeping her legs together and placing my knees on the outside of hers, I thrust my cock inside her and held myself still, buried to the hilt. "So, my little milkmaid, you have shown me what you can do with your pretty little mouth, and now you shall milk my cock again. I want you to pull and squeeze and milk me dry again, and I shall remain still and observe your efforts, which I expect to be both enthusiastic and creative." When Betsy didn't respond after a moment, I gave her ass a small pinch and demanded, "And how do you answer respectfully?"

"Yes, my Lord," she responded meekly, making me grin with satisfaction.

And so it began, Betsy clenching her inner muscles around me, rocking her body forward and then leaning it back to take me all the way in.

"Yes, that's…it…my sweet. Very…good," I encouraged her. Then I went silent so I could enjoy both the sight and the sensations of her working my cock, which she did with an expertise I found momentarily disturbing. I gazed rapt at the sight as my length disappeared and reappeared with her slow movements. It was amazing, which was a bit surprising considering I normally needed to have control. But again it pleased me to compel her to further her own debasement.

I was still enjoying myself, so much so that I felt confident in both my ability and desire to continue indefinitely. But having used Betsy so abominably earlier, it seemed only courteous to hasten the end. And so I took over, grabbing Betsy's luscious ass and holding her steady while I began to pound my cock inside her, moving faster and faster, lunging harder, building steadily to my release. I came with a savage cry, exploding with pleasure, and twitching as her muscles did indeed milk me dry.

I collapsed next to Betsy and cuddled up behind her, planting grateful kisses on her shoulders as I relaxed. When my breathing had resumed its normal pace, I whispered in her ear, "My dear, you are far too talented to be a milkmaid. How would you like to be my chambermaid instead?"

"With pleasure, my Lord," I heard her sigh.

TEA FOR TWO

BY JOY FULCHER

"It sure is quiet tonight, Claire," I said, staring at the empty tables in the pub. "Where is everyone?"

Claire shrugged her shoulders and took a long draw on her cigarette. "There's a rally in town tonight. John Adams is giving a speech about being free from British oppression."

"Do you really think that's possible?"

"I pray that it is, child." Claire smiled and blew smoke toward me. Her face had aged well, considering she was nearing fifty years old, and her body was still one of the most requested by the clientele.

"Stop sitting about and do some work. If there's no men around then get to cleanin'!" Mr. Brown, the saloon owner, snapped from behind the bar.

There were three of us working tonight, waiting and ready to comfort the wealthy men of Boston. It just appeared that no men were seeking comfort this night. We all rushed around the room, straightening chairs and wiping the already clean tables, doing anything we could to keep busy. None of us could risk the wrath of Mr. Brown — we all needed the pay.

"Is your brother home, May?" Bridget whispered as we both fussed over the flower arrangement near the door, picking dead leaves from their stems.

"He'll be home tomorrow. Shall I tell him that you asked after him?"

"Heavens no! He'd think me too forward. But, perhaps I could stop by for tea in the afternoon?"

I smiled. It was no secret that Bridget was enamored with my brother, Henry. He often came to drink at the pub, and I'd noticed him giving her the eye a few times.

"Of course. Mother would love to have you over," I told her.

Bridget gave me a grateful smile and moved to dust the mantle over the hearth.

"Did ya' hear? Did ya'll hear?"

Everyone froze and turned to look at the small boy who'd just run through the door. His clothes were ripped and there was a streak of dirt across his face.

"Hear what, Duncan?" Mr. Brown asked the boy.

"There's a raid happnin' at the docks! A bunch of savages are throwing all the cargo off the ships into the water!"

"Don't you be spreading such lies, boy," Mr. Brown grumbled.

"It's true, mister. I heard a policeman yell for people to stay away from the docks until they caught them Indians." With that, Duncan turned and ran out into the street. We could hear him calling to strangers as he ran down the block.

"Are we in danger?" Bridget gasped.

"Nonsense. It's nonsense. We haven't had In'jins in the heart of town in years. Ya'll get back to work," he barked.

Bridget rushed over to me, her skirts swirling around her legs.

"Do you think it's true, May?" she whispered.

I waited until Mr. Brown has his back turned and then crept over to the window to look outside. The streets were dark. I could see the tall masts from the ships docked in the bay rising over the waterfront buildings, but being three streets back from the docks, I couldn't see any commotion.

"Who knows," I said, with a shrug of my shoulders.

"I said, back to work! May, don't try me tonight if you want to keep your job."

I hung my head. "Yes, Mr. Brown."

When he turned his back again, Bridget poked her tongue at him, but I waved her gesture away and shook my head. I didn't want her to get in trouble as well.

Claire put a hand on my arm and ushered me away from the window. "Come on girls, let's get some—"

Suddenly, the doors burst open and a dozen savages came into the room. They were all yelling and laughing as their feathered head-dresses bobbed with their movements.

Bridget screamed and clung to my arm.

"In'jins aren't welcome here," Mr. Brown boomed, puffing his chest out and reaching under the bar to pull out his musket.

"Fear not, barkeep," a man with a distinctly proper Boston accent said, pushing his way through the Indians. He was dressed in a handsome suit and tricorn hat.

"Mr. Adams," Claire gasped.

Mr. Brown dropped the barrel of his gun but still eyed the feathered men warily.

"We are but Americans, like yourself," John Adams said, pulling the headdress off a young man standing beside him. The young man's sandy blond hair stuck up in all directions, and I felt myself physically relax, seeing that the hair underneath wasn't inky black. "This is my son, Joseph."

"Come in, Mr. Adams," Mr. Brown said warmly. He pulled several glasses off a shelf and started to pour ale for the men.

The crowd in the doorway all seated themselves around the room and removed their headwear. The faces of white-skinned men smiled at Bridget, Claire, and myself. Bridget let go of my arms and swayed her hips as she walked across the room.

"You all but scared the life outta me," she taunted one of the men before sitting in his lap.

An hour later, the men had regaled us all with the tale of their adventure on board the ships docked in the harbor. We cheered as they described sneaking aboard the ships and throwing the crates of tea into the dark water as a protest to King George's tea tax. It was nearing midnight, and the men were still celebrating their victory over oppression.

"We won't pay King George his taxes. Not in my lifetime!" one of the men roared.

That was followed by a chorus of "Here, here!" and more drinking.

John Adams stood up, and everyone fell silent.

"For obvious reasons of propriety, I could not participate with you in your victory on the ship, but please know that I support you." Mr. Adams turned to Mr. Brown who was still behind the bar. "Barkeep. Another round of drinks for these brave men, on me."

He walked over and dropped several coins onto the bar before bidding the men goodnight and leaving the pub. Bridget, Claire, and I all hurried to gather the new round of drinks and distribute them among the already intoxicated men.

"Thank you," Joseph Adams said as I handed him his drink. He looked a lot like his father, and I guessed his age to be about twenty. His eyes shone in the flickering candlelight, and he gave me a lopsided grin. "What's your name?"

I bowed my head. "May Greenwood."

"It's a pleasure to meet you, Miss Greenwood. Could I have the pleasure of your company for a while?"

"Of course."

I quickly handed out the rest of the drinks from my tray and made my way back to Joseph.

"Mr. Adams," I said, holding my hand out to him.

Some of the other men whistled and cheered as he took my hand and stood up. He winked to the man sitting beside him and then slung his arm over my shoulder in a very familiar way. I knew that a lady should never let a man she didn't know touch her in such a casual manner, but he was paying for my time — time to do whatever he wished with me — so I had little choice.

I led Joseph to the bar and gave Mr. Brown a wink, our signal that I'd been requested.

"Pay first," Mr. Brown said, barely looking up from his task of polishing the clean glasses.

Joseph dug in his pocket and placed several coins on the counter.

"Room three," Mr. Brown said with a nod of his head.

I turned and led Joseph up the stairs to room three, closing the door behind us. All the upstairs rooms were the same. A small area with peeling flowered wallpaper, a wash stand, a fireplace, and a bed. The beds were the only new things in the room. Mr. Brown had recently sprung for new straw mattresses and twisted iron bedposts.

I took in Joseph's face as he scanned the room. He looked a fright with his costume on, but I suspected that there was a handsome man underneath. The next hour would be a much nicer experience than my usual night at work with older gentlemen who had wives at home waiting up for them.

"Would you care to wash up?" I offered, going to collect the large jug of water from its place by the fire where it had been set earlier in the night to warm up.

"Thank you." He shrugged out of his vest and calfskin boots.

I poured the steaming water into the washstand's basin.

"Thank you, May," he said, coming up behind me and dipping his hands in the water.

He rubbed the war paint off his face and let out a sigh. "That stuff is itchy on your skin, you know," he said, smirking.

I was taken aback by how handsome Joseph was now that his face was his own, without feathers and paint. His blond hair and blue eyes were striking.

"Shall I undress for you, sir?" I asked, looking quickly down at the ground when he caught me staring at him.

His hands clasped my shoulders and pulled me to him. "Please, call me Joseph. And could I do the honors?"

I nodded. He was close, and I could feel the warmth coming off his body. His skin smelled like ocean air and tea leaves. It was intoxicating, and I breathed in a little deeper as my eyes fluttered shut.

I felt my dress fall away from my shoulders and pool around my feet.

"Well, you are a pretty thing," Joseph said approvingly.

"You smell like tea," I whispered.

He laughed and I opened my eyes to see that he was rummaging in his pocket.

"I think this is your culprit," he admitted, pulling out a handful of loose leaves and showing them to me. The spicy smell intensified in the room that was a little too hot from the fire.

"I thought you threw it all in the water?" I asked.

"Most of it. I kept a little for myself." He shrugged his shoulders and put the leaves back in his pocket. "But I'm more interested in you than in the tea."

His hands reached for me, and I stepped toward him, allowing him to lead me to the bed.

"How shall I please you?" I asked.

"By allowing me to please you," he whispered. "I've heard my friend speak of an act that is done in India. I've been dying to try it. They call it *cunnilingus*...Have you heard of it?"

"I have not," I said, gawking at the strange word.

"May I?"

"Will it hurt me?" I knew he was paying for this time and it was my duty to allow him to take his pleasure from me, but I was a little afraid.

Joseph chuckled. "The exact opposite. The purpose is to give you pleasure."

"All right." I was still wary, but so rarely did I gain any pleasure from this work that I couldn't help but be intrigued. I'd heard other comfort women say that with some men, they felt an intense physical pleasure. I had yet to experience that. It would be a welcome change.

"Lie down," he encouraged, and I did as I was asked.

I kicked off my shoes and lay, naked, on the bed. Joseph crawled across the bed, still clothed, and lay over me.

"I promise you'll like this," he murmured as his lips descended on mine.

The kiss was nice but I didn't feel any physical pleasure. Our mouths moved against each other, tongues stroking, as his hands moved over my shoulder and down to my rib cage.

"Your skin is softer than I imagined," he said into my mouth.

"Is that good?"

"Very. Just with so many men touching you, I would have imagined it to be rougher."

I pulled back. It was one thing to be a whore, and another to be insulted for it.

"I'm sorry, sir, but..."

His mouth descended on mine again, his body pressing mine down into the straw mattress.

"I meant no disrespect, May. I think you are beautiful," he murmured with a gravelly voice. "Just try to relax."

His request was impossible. My body remained tense as his hands moved over my flesh, kneading and stroking at my skin. Gradually, his whole body slid down mine. His lips trailing kisses first over my throat, then down to my bosom and over my belly. I'd never had a man spend so much time kissing me, and in so many varied places! When Claire had trained me, she'd never mentioned anything about having a man lick her bellybutton.

Despite the oddness of the activity, I found it quite pleasurable, just as Joseph had promised. My skin felt on fire everywhere he touched, and the heat began to build in my belly in a way that it never had before.

I tilted my head and stared between the valley of my breasts at the mop of golden hair moving over my body. There was something strangely arousing about seeing him there.

"What are you doing?" I gasped. He had moved lower, pressing his mouth into the soft flesh between my legs. "Don't!"

I tried to pull away, pushing at his head with my hand, but he held firmly to my hips so I couldn't squirm.

"Trust me, May. I'm not going to hurt you."

"You want to kiss me *there?*" I couldn't fathom it.

"Very much."

Before I had a chance to question why, his mouth was on me. His tongue probing my most private of places.

I gasped with a mixture of shock and pleasure. Joseph hadn't lied — it felt very good. I'd never imagined my body was capable of producing such a sensation. He licked and sucked without stopping for quite a while as my hips started to jerk back and forth without my control.

Warmth and euphoria flooded through my body slowly. Starting at my core and flowing incessantly down my legs until my toes curled and my legs wound around Joseph, holding him to me. My breathing was ragged, and still Joseph did not relent.

"What…what is happening?" I cried out as violent waves cascaded through my body and my hips lifted off the bed. It was as if a volcano had erupted inside my body. I was soaring, gliding through the heavens and then, just as quickly as it started, I found myself sprawled back on the bed, gasping for breath.

I had no idea what had just happened. All I knew was that it was the most pleasurable moment of my life and I wished to experience it many more times.

"Joseph," I panted. "What did you do to me?"

He crawled up my body and collapsed on his side, next to me, wearing a lazy grin.

"Was it very pleasurable?" he asked.

"Extremely," I assured him.

"Good. One day, when I take a wife, I plan to pleasure her in that manner."

I smiled and ran my fingers through his hair. "You are most welcome to practice on me whenever you wish."

He laughed. "All in the name of up-skilling me to provide a better experience for my future wife?"

I blushed. "Of course."

"Have you ever performed *fellatio* on a man?"

"I wouldn't even know what that was," I admitted, feeling a little silly.

"May, if it's not too impolite to ask, what usually happens in this room?"

I sat up and curled my legs to my chest. "Well, I give men pleasure with my body."

"What parts of your body?" His hand ran down my bare back, trailing shivers along my spine.

"With...you know, where you just had your mouth."

"Only there?"

"Of course. Isn't that the purpose of a whore?"

He ignored my question and just continued to run his fingers up and down my back.

"Have you ever thought of using your mouth on a man, just as I just did for you?"

"Never," I admitted. "Would that be pleasurable for you?"

"I have never experienced it, but I believe it would be."

"Do you wish for me to try?"

"Very much."

I was acutely aware of the fact that I was completely naked, and apart from his boots lying on the floor, Joseph was still fully dressed. I reached for him, and he allowed me to unbutton his shirt and push it over his shoulders.

The tea leaves from his pockets spilled onto the bed and scattered through the ripples in the sheet.

"Oh, I'm so sorry."

"Never mind that," he said, shrugging the shirt off his shoulders and dropping it to the floor. I eyed his belt and reached for it, but he beat me to it and quickly removed his pants, discarding them to where his shirt fell.

His manhood was stiff, something I was accustomed to, but I'd never been faced with putting my face near to it before.

"How do I do it?"

Joseph cupped my cheek and looked into my eyes.

"Do you enjoy candies?"

"I love them!"

"Just do what you would do with a candy. Lick and suck."

I nodded and slid down his body, my nipples rubbing over his chest and stomach. He was almost hairless except for a small spattering of blond in the center of his chest. The musky scent of man wafted from his skin and mixed with the strong smell of tea that floated up from the spilled leaves on the mattress. It was intoxicating.

I lay on my stomach between his legs and studied his manhood. I sized up how to approach the unfamiliar task and decided to just dive in. I'd eaten plenty of candies, enough to know how to eat one skillfully.

I giggled to myself, marveling at how many men I had given pleasure to in my months as a whore and yet, I'd never held a man's member in my hand. The usual time spent with a man was quick and to the point. Most of them didn't even undress me. Most nights, I didn't even bother to wear undergarments under my dress. They just slowed down the proceedings. I was used to having my skirts lifted and then the man would push inside me and take his pleasure.

It wasn't uncomfortable or painful, but on very few occasions had I felt anything that even resembled pleasure, let alone what I'd felt with Joseph's mouth down there. What an awakening.

Remembering my own pleasure from a moment ago, I wished to give Joseph the same sensation and grabbed his shaft, stroking it firmly. He let out a soft hum and closed his eyes. I stroked a few more times before daring to move my face forward. His scent was stronger this close; I could almost taste it as I extended my tongue and hesitantly licked the tip.

I hadn't expected it to taste like anything—like licking a finger—but it did. It tasted like nothing I'd ever had before, and I couldn't explain it to myself. It was salty and also sweet. It didn't taste good but not altogether bad either. I licked again and glanced up Joseph's body to see him watching me with wide eyes and a half smile.

"Go on," he whispered.

I focused my attention between his legs again and took him into my mouth, engulfing the entire head. Joseph's response was unexpected, and I gagged as his hips pushed him deeper, almost into my throat. I coughed and pulled away, my cheeks burning with shame.

"I'm sorry," I choked out.

"Are you all right?" he asked, sitting up, his eyes soft with concern.

"Yes, I just was not expecting you to thrust forward in such a manner. I'll do better."

I moved my mouth over him again, taking him in, but he didn't lie back down. He stayed seated, leaning back on his arms, and looked down at me as I moved my mouth up and down the shaft. I took extra care not to allow the tip to hit the back of my throat again, but once I built up a rhythm, the task became quite simple.

Joseph moved one hand forward and threaded it into my hair, guiding my mouth as I moved over him. He was mostly silent except for a soft grunt or gasp of breath, but the constant spasms of his hips let me know that he was close to losing himself over to the pleasure.

Not wanting to risk him ramming the back of my throat again when he lost control, I made the quick decision to finish off by hand. I was aware of how violently the male release occurred and didn't fancy the idea of it happening inside my mouth.

I pulled my head away and started up a brisk motion with both of my hands, massaging the stiff flesh. I looked at Joseph's face and saw that his eyes were scrunched closed. I took that as a good sign, as I had seen many men pull a similar expression when they were close to release.

My hand pumped furiously as his hips pushed up and held still in the air. Spurts of his release fell onto his stomach, and I watched in awe. I'd never actually seen a man's release before, as it always happened inside me. I continued to stroke until he fell against the bed, gasping for breath.

"Was that what you hoped for?" I asked, crawling up the bed and lying next to him as his chest continued to rise and fall.

He laughed. "My only wish is that I can find a wife half as skilled as you are, May. That was magnificent."

"It is my pleasure to serve." I smiled at him but noticed that he was frowning. "What is wrong?"

"I don't suppose I will find such a wife. What noble woman would ever pleasure me with her mouth? It wouldn't be proper."

I thought for a moment. "That might be the case, but many married men visit me here. I would be happy to continue to meet with you like this."

"And what of your future husband? Do you think he will share you with me?"

I laughed. "I don't hold much hope for a husband, sir. What man would marry a woman of my background? I expect I'll know many men in my life, and none of them will belong to me. They will all go home to their wives, just as you will."

His face softened. "I believe there is a man who would love you and forget your past."

"Perhaps. There is always hope, I suppose. But, I don't allow myself to dream of it, lest my life turn into a nightmare."

"Perhaps I could be that man," he offered, his eyes sparkling.

I laughed again and stroked my fingers over his chest.

"You are only charmed by me because of the pleasure I just gave your body. When the blood rushes back to your brain, you will see sense. The least of the problems with that suggestion would be the opinion of your father. Such an important man could never have a whore for a daughter-in-law."

Joseph frowned. "You are right, of course. He would never allow it. But I may still enjoy you for tonight." He gave a devilish grin and flipped us over so that he was lying over the top of me.

It was such an exhilaration to feel his bare skin on mine. The most common position I'd experienced was bent over the foot of the bed with my skirt flipped over my head. The only skin I was used to feeling was a man's thighs bumping against the back of my legs as he moved behind me. Having a man's chest and stomach pressed against my own was so much more intimate than I was accustomed to, and I liked it.

"Yes, you may enjoy me," I agreed, spreading my legs for him.

He pushed inside and seated himself firmly, not moving, just staring into my eyes.

"Perhaps I could convince my father…" he started, but I kissed his lips to cut off his words. We both knew there was no chance his father would ever approve of me. But the fact that he'd said the words at all meant a lot to me. I would show him my appreciation with my body. It was the only way I could.

I wrapped my legs around his hips, tilting my pelvis to take him as deep as possible. He needed no further encouragement than that and began to rock against me. The air in the room was warm and the closeness of Joseph's body to my own caused my skin to feel sticky. The tea leaves scattered across the bed stuck to my back and arms as we rocked on the bed. He began moving in longer strokes, pulling in and out at a slow pace. His head fell against my shoulder, and I wrapped my arms around him, pulling him as close to my body as possible. His breath was loud and heavy against my throat.

"Are you enjoying me, Joseph?" I asked.

"Sweet, May. I've never enjoyed anything more."

His thrusting increased, building the pressure inside my body. The good feeling was intense but not the same as the concentrated pleasure of Joseph's mouth. His lips found mine and he kissed me deeply, probing my mouth with his own. He exhaled, our breath mixing together while he sucked and nibbled at my bottom lip.

Our movements were growing more and more frantic. Joseph broke the kiss and I mewled at the loss of contact with his mouth. His face hovered just above my own, holding me with his gaze as he continued the unbroken rhythm of his hips. I was swallowed up by the blue of his eyes, the smell of the tea, the feel of his arms around me, and his skin against mine. It was sensory overload as I fell into heaven and my muscles convulsed around him while I cried out his name.

"Beautiful May," he grunted and then kissed me again.

My pleasure didn't stop with release. He continued to race toward his own pleasure and I rocked underneath him, helping as much as I could to get him there. His hands snaked down between our bodies and caressed my breasts, pinching the nipples and kneading the mounds.

"Every part of you is so soft," he said with a low breath, struggling to get the words out.

I ran my hands down the tight muscles of his back, taut from the exertion of his movements.

"And every part of you is so hard."

We both laughed, the movement of our laughter rocking our bodies together harder than before. He certainly was hard, in all the right ways.

He dropped his head to my shoulder again and rested there while he pounded his hips, moving harder and faster than before. When he lifted his neck to look at me, he had tea leaves stuck to his forehead, I giggled and leaned up to kiss them off his skin.

He looked at me curiously as I poked out my tongue, showing him the leaves. He grinned and kissed me, sucking my tongue into his mouth. The taste of the tea was intense as we kissed.

A loud banging on the door shocked us both and we froze.

"Time's up!" Mr. Brown called through the door.

"Another hour," Joseph called. "I'll pay you when I come back downstairs."

I could hear Mr. Brown grumbling as his footsteps moved away from the door, but couldn't make out what he was saying.

"It's been an hour already," Joseph said, his voice sad, his movements stilled.

"Are you certain you don't mind paying more? I could finish you off quickly and am sure I could convince Mr. Brown not to charge you for a few extra minutes."

"No, May. I want the hour. I'm taking my time with you, remember? Enjoying my girl."

I giggled. "Well, please do continue to enjoy me, sir."

"Would you…"

"Anything, Joseph."

"Would you take the lead?" His eyes fell to the floor and he refused to look at me.

"Gladly." I hugged him close as he pulled out from between my legs and then crawled over him as he lay on his back. I swung my leg over his hips and sat down, encompassing his manhood inside of me.

He let out a soft grunt and stared up at me with wonder in his eyes. The candle on the nightstand provided a flickering light that danced in his eyes as I moved over him. I was not well-practiced at this new position, as most men preferred to take me from behind or to be on top as Joseph had just been, but my movements felt natural, as if my body knew what to do.

I rocked over him, his hands roaming over my breasts and stomach.

"I've never seen anything as beautiful as you, in this moment in the moonlight," he said with a sigh.

I glanced over my shoulder to the open window and saw that the moonlight was bathing the floor and the bed, casting a silver glow over my skin.

I was lost in the romance of the moment. A beautiful man who expressed wishes for a life of us together—even if that wish was futile—the moonlight mixed with the flickering candlelight, and the aroma of the tea. I'd never had a night like it.

"I'm getting close, May. Will you climax again with me?"

"You want me to?" I asked.

"Yes. Very much." His words were labored, and I wondered if he was holding back his own release, waiting for me.

I wouldn't keep him waiting any longer. I slammed my body down on his as hard as I could and reached my hand down to a special place that brought me pleasure. Joseph had found it during the cunnilingus. I was unsure if every woman had that tiny bulb of pleasure—I'd never had the nerve to ask the other girls downstairs—but I knew that if I touched it, my release would be swift.

He watched my hand with a half-open mouth as I rubbed between my legs while still moving over him. It was a difficult combination of moves to keep in rhythm, but my body knew what it was doing.

My body exploded in pleasure and I cried out, gasping for breath as waves of intense heat pulsed through me. In what sounded like the distance, I heard Joseph cry out as well, cursing words that a lady should never hear, interspersed with my name, over and over. I felt the familiar sensation of his seed filling me, warm and wet, and then we were both silent, but still breathing heavily.

He reached his arms up and pulled me down to lay across his chest and peppered kisses on my face.

"You are a wondrous creature, Miss May."

"As are you, Joseph."

He held me tightly against him, stroking his fingertips over my damp skin.

"We could be like this forever, May. Let me speak with my father."

I pulled back and looked down at him.

"Why would you want to do that? I am just a comfort girl."

Joseph blushed, his cheeks and throat flushing with red.

"I've seen you before tonight. Many times. I've watched you in the marketplace buying vegetables for your family. I've seen you walking with your brother in town. I've desired you, May."

My mouth dropped open. I'd had no idea that Joseph had seen me. I knew who *he* was, of course. As the son of one of the most influential men in the country, he was known to most people in Boston, but for him to notice me? I felt shocked.

"Joseph, you sweet man. There is a girl out there with blood as noble as your own, waiting for a handsome young man to woo her and ask for her hand. She will be as pure as snow and know only your touch, unlike me who has been touched by many. That is the life you are meant to lead."

"Perhaps. But it is not the life I want." He pressed a kiss to my shoulder and smiled. "Your skin tastes like tea."

I pondered for a moment. "You know, many people will rejoice in what you did tonight on those ships. Throwing the tea into the harbor was a bold statement to send to King George. But, in all honesty, I'll miss drinking tea."

Joseph laughed a deep belly laughed that echoed around the room. He threw his head back, and I smiled to see him so happy. He leaned forward and pressed his lips to my ear.

"Don't tell anyone," he whispered. "But I hid one of the crates. My mother loves tea and I wanted to save her some. I shall bring a portion to you. The stores will run out very quickly so it may be the last tea in all of Boston."

"You don't have to do that."

"I want to. You can think of me every time you enjoy a cup."

"Shall I enjoy it the way you enjoyed me?" I teased, nudging him with my shoulder.

He laughed again. "I doubt anyone could enjoy a mere cup of tea quite that much."

My heart was warm, being in this private space with Joseph. My mind played over his request to allow him to ask his father about being with me. I knew I couldn't let him do it, but for just a moment, I allowed myself to picture a future with the Adams family. I was sure it would be a happy life.

Joseph must have noticed the frown that had formed on my face because he cocked his head to the side and reached over to lift my chin so I was staring him in the eye.

"Is all well, May?"

"Oh, yes. I'm sorry. But, we should get you dressed and downstairs before Mr. Brown comes banging on the door again."

Joseph frowned too. "Very well."

We both dressed in silence, and I took a moment to brush the discarded tea leaves from the bed onto the floor, kicking them underneath. I'd sweep them up after Joseph had left. I looked up to see him standing by the door, his hand poised over the handle. He turned back to me.

"Do you remember when I asked if I could practice cunnilingus on you?"

"So you'll know better how to pleasure your future wife. Of course."

He chewed his lip. "How would it be if I kept that as something that only we do together? I am sure whatever waif of an heiress my father deems worthy to be my bride would have heart failure if I tried to do it with her."

He chuckled, but his eyes were intense.

"Like a secret affair?"

"If you wish to call it that. I may be forced to give my name to another, but I'm offering my heart to you."

"Your heart?"

"If you'll accept it. I will visit you weekly and we shall drink tea and make love."

I nodded my head, holding in the tears that stung my eyes.

He grinned and left the room, closing the door behind him. I clutched my arms to my chest and spun in a circle, my skirts swirling around me. I turned and ran back to the bed, crouching down to scoop some tea leaves from the floor and inhaling deeply. Forevermore, I would think of this night with Joseph whenever I smelled a good cup of tea.

I knew how important it was and how deserving we were of our independence. I believed that we would be strong as an independent nation. But I certainly was going to miss the tea.

E. PLURIBUS THREESOME

BY KIMBERLY JENSEN & SCOTT STARK

Historical prologue: Alexander Hamilton spent the summer of 1773 at the home of colonial luminary William Livingston, one of the most influential politicians of the Revolutionary Era. While residing at Livingston's grand estate, he became acquainted with the remarkable Livingston daughters, most notably Catharine, or "Kitty" as she was known to family and close friends. There was, at the very least, a shared attraction between Alexander and Kitty, though a relationship of a sexual nature is more likely, based on the content and tone of letters sent between them during the Revolution. What is also clear is that Kitty Livingston introduced Alexander Hamilton to Elizabeth Schuyler, his future wife.

"**B**loody hell," Alexander mumbled as he made his way through the Elizabethtown streets. Despite the oppressive summer heat, his steps were purposeful and quick. Galas at the Livingston estate were not to be missed and punctuality was preferred.

Alexander had decided long ago that although William Livingston was nauseatingly wealthy, he was also a good man. When Alexander was a penniless orphan of limited means, Livingston had taken him in almost as if he were another son, then offered his good name to help him obtain admission to King's College. His time with the brilliant, gregarious Livingston brood had taught him a great deal about life and society.

As he walked, his thoughts wandered to Livingston's bright-eyed, quick-witted youngest daughter, Kitty. The way she looked at him through her thick fringe of lashes made Alexander's pulse quicken. She was no stranger to men, yet skillfully managed her reputation so any notions of her libertine nature were not suspected by polite society.

He placed his hand to the breast pocket of his summer coat and felt the letter he'd received that morning.

Mister Hamilton,

I pray I can expect you at Papa's little soirée this evening. It shall be quite fun and full of dazzling people. I do so want you to make the acquaintance of my dearest friend, Miss Elizabeth Schuyler. You will be quite taken with her, I am sure. Her father is Major General Philip Schuyler, a good connection for you, I think.

Hamilton, I should think it quite pleasurable if you could stay a bit with me after all the usual revelers take their leave. You need not respond, but if you were to thrice rap upon the door of my bed chamber, I should be quite happy, as will you, I promise.

Your Kitty

Catharine, Kitty to her family, was the most captivating woman he'd ever met. Her dark eyes hinted at sharp intelligence, and she had a gift for turning even the simplest action—raising her cup, for instance—into an overtly sexual one. She had first seduced him when he moved into her family home, the very grand Liberty Hall. He'd been sleeping wearing no clothing during the hot New Jersey summer and awakened to her standing before him in the darkened room in all her bare, goddess-like glory.

They shared a genuine friendship, but occasionally they shared more. School kept him busy, and she offered a welcome respite.

Alexander's pace quickened as he approached the main house.

The grand table ran nearly the length of the dining room. The ornate settings, resplendent with fine crystal and china, were outshone only by the luminaries present. Livingston himself sat at the head of the table, flanked on his right by Alexander's morose and brilliant friend John Jay and on his left by an older gentleman with a patrician air and dark, intelligent eyes. Despite the lavish arrangements, the mood in the room was easy and informal. Alexander stepped into view.

"Hamilton!" boomed Livingston, standing as he spoke. "Come here, lad! You must meet my friend Schuyler!"

"Major General?" Alexander crossed the room in a few long steps and extended his hand in greeting. Schuyler took Alexander's hand in both of his own and shook purposefully.

"I've heard much about you, Mr. Hamilton. I'm pleased to finally meet the man taking King's College by storm!"

"Perhaps not by storm; probably not even one lightning strike at a time," quipped Alexander. Pleasantries were exchanged all around and eventually further greetings with other guests were traded. There were, of course, Mrs. Livingston and all the Livingston daughters, including the ever-bewitching Kitty.

"Mister Hamilton, please meet Major General Schuyler's daughter Elizabeth. Elizabeth, do acquaint yourself with our dearest friend, Alexander Hamilton. You will find him quite charming, I promise." Kitty's introduction was effervescent.

Elizabeth leveled a direct gaze at Alexander and took his extended hand. The touch was brief, but the jolt of sensual reaction was unmistakable. She dipped in a small, graceful curtsy and resumed her seat. Her eyes, nearly black, lingered on his far longer than necessary or proper. Hamilton, almost imperceptibly speechless for a moment following the electricity exchanged with Elizabeth, was assigned a seat between his spectacularly attractive friend and his alluring new acquaintance.

As expected, the lively conversation turned to politics. Mere weeks before, the Parliament of Great Britain passed the Tea Act designed to save the British East India Company by granting it a monopoly on the North American tea trade. Like most colonists with ties, financial and otherwise, to merchants and importers, most at the table rejected the Act.

"The Act is odious not so much because it rescues the East India Company, but because it validates the Townshend tax on tea. Legal importers stand to lose their business, as do those whose business will be undercut by the Company's lowered prices," Elizabeth opined.

Damn. Such a mind in such a body, thought Alexander.

"All I know is that only one thing could make this sumptuous meal exceed all others ever consumed." Kitty sighed, then paused before continuing. "A cup of tea."

The table laughed at the opportunity to break into informal banter following heavy talk of government policy and several small conversations began amongst the guests as wine was poured and continually refilled.

While the rest of the partygoers were involved in conversations of their own, Kitty leaned into Alexander and seductively spoke in a low voice that was not quite a whisper. "You will visit me tonight, yes?"

Alexander turned his gaze to Kitty with mock indignation before the corners of his mouth rose ever so slightly. "I will consider it," he answered, though his eyes said *yes*. They lingered on one another a moment longer as visitors began to take their leave or to retire upstairs.

"Alexander," Kitty inquired in the same close, sensual voice, "will you mind so much if we are joined by a dear friend?"

Alexander crept toward Kitty's sleeping chamber, already aroused by the notion that Elizabeth might be able to join them for a while. *Ahh, Miss Elizabeth*, he thought, *why am I so taken with someone I know so little about?* What untold beauty lay in store? He did not know but certainly was keen to remedy that.

He was there, ostensibly, for Kitty. He knew that. A pleasant memory of their last fleshly congress overtook him for a moment: Her long raven hair had spilled down her back like fine runlets and ebbed once they approached the inviting curvature of her hips. She'd flashed him a wicked smile that had told him everything he'd needed to know. *Come to me. Come to me and show me pleasure.* It was all there, indelibly etched in the gray matter of his memory.

He knocked the previously agreed upon three times.

The door swung open.

"Mister Hamilton." Kitty smiled. "Please, do come in."

Kitty, wearing only her silk chemise, stepped aside, allowing Alexander passage. The room was dimly lit with only the smallest of candles. He could smell the bouquet of a fine wine waft past his face as he embraced Kitty and kissed her gently.

"I hope I'm not interrupting, sir," a voice from the corner of the room whispered.

It was Elizabeth, sitting on Kitty's bed. She held two glasses of a nicely aged claret in her hands. She was dressed in a gossamer shift so fine that Alexander marveled at the way it somehow revealed so little while still showing so much. Kitty moved toward Elizabeth and took one of the glasses from her delicate hand.

"Will you join us for some wine, then?"

Yes. He would. Without a doubt.

"My ladies. Both of you. So beautiful tonight."

They both giggled, cheeks blossoming. He took an empty glass from the corner table and filled it with the sweet nectar.

"Excellent wine, madams."

"Thank you, Mr. Hamilton. It is a favorite of mine," Elizabeth replied. She smiled coquettishly and looked to her lap.

"Alexander, why are you standing so far away? Come join us," Kitty cooed, patting her pillow.

He crossed the room and sat on the bed between the two women. He began kissing Kitty while putting his hand on Elizabeth's left thigh. Elizabeth jumped, let out a little shriek, and bolted from the bed.

"Sir...sir, I do not wish to offend, but I—"

"No, madam. It is I who should apologize." Alexander got up from the bed and offered her a hand. She shrank at the offer.

"Alexander, my dear Lizzy merely wishes to watch. She is beautiful, isn't she? What do you say?" Kitty was lying on her back on the bed, her chemise cinched up to just above mid-thigh.

Elizabeth blushed and looked away from both of them.

"Is this true, Elizabeth? Do you wish to watch us together?" Alexander asked. He had to admit that the idea of this beautiful creature wanting to view him buried within Kitty's warm walls was tantalizing.

Elizabeth balked, her gaze fixed on the window outside.

"I am not wholly naïve, Mister Hamilton. I've experienced one or two brief dalliances, but they were uninspired and lacking in passion. I suspect there is much I don't know and much more to be enjoyed, I...merely need to learn." Elizabeth paused, then turned to Alexander.

"I do love it here in summer. It's so...so, lovely," she offered nervously.

"What? I'm sorry?" Alexander asked as Kitty smiled from the other end of the bed.

"Yes. Yes, I wish to watch."

"All right, then."

"But, sir, not the whole time. Just for a little while."

"All right, then."

Alexander removed his silk waistcoat and released himself from the tight breeches that left little to the imagination, all the while staring straight at Elizabeth. She returned his gaze and began to rub herself beneath her slip at the sight of his nakedness. Alexander turned toward Kitty and slinked up toward her on the bed.

"Thank you, from both of us." Kitty smiled and met his embrace as they kissed passionately. Alexander pushed up the chemise, exposing her hips and cunny to all of creation.

Elizabeth let out a soft sigh and began touching herself with more urgency.

Kitty pulled Alexander into her. He straightened his legs and supported his weight on either side of her with locked arms. His stroke quickened and he turned his head to watch Elizabeth. She had managed to push the functional portion of her shift aside and was pleasuring herself with complete abandon.

"Look at me. Look at me, Alexander," Kitty pleaded as he thrust himself deeper inside her. He turned to face Kitty, lovely Kitty, who had been so generous this summer with her carnality.

He brushed her breast with his left hand and gently licked the other with a searching tongue. Then his body suddenly stilled and he shuddered. Kitty wrapped her legs around his torso and hissed his name over and over. The veins bulged from Alexander's neck as he came in a rush of mumbled moans and words he would forget in the morning.

"Yes! Yes! Yes!" Kitty screamed. Alexander turned to where Elizabeth had been sitting.

But she was gone.

"Where—"

"It's all right, Alexander. She saw all she wanted." Kitty sighed.

"I never even heard her leave."

Kitty laughed. Alexander scrutinized her face.

"You are smitten, aren't you?" she asked.

"Certainly not. Though, she is beautiful, I will admit."

"She is also my best friend in this world."

Alexander sighed and laid back down on the bed, looking at the emptiness of the blanched ceiling.

"Oh, don't sulk, Alexander. She likes you. And I like that she likes you."

Alexander's face lit up as a smile emerged, flooding his otherwise serious countenance.

"She likes me?"

"Yes, you utter dolt. She likes you." Kitty punched him on the arm then, and they both broke out in wild fits of laughter.

Alexander steeled himself and rapped upon the door. Long moments later, it was opened by a stern looking maid with a dour face and a white cap that, no matter how crisp, looked frumpy on her head.

"I'm here to see Miss Elizabeth," Alexander announced.

The housekeeper glared at him disapprovingly. "Who may I tell her is calling?"

"Alexander Hamilton," he replied, his gaze cool and direct enough for her to instantly comprehend he was not a man to disregard. She nodded once, curtly, and directed him through the large door and into a large, open entry hall.

His conversation with Elizabeth at their first meeting prepared him for a lively household — there were, after all, fifteen Schuyler children — but the activity within the smallish mansion surprised him. It was less neat than he imagined; there were books left on tables, and chairs were not perfectly arranged. Clearly, people frequently came, pulled up a chair to chat, and went away. In the background, Alexander heard indistinct noises too numerous to isolate. It was the sound of nearly two dozen people going about their lives.

"You'll wait here," the maid instructed as she gestured at the door to a parlor. "I will inform Miss Elizabeth you are here to see her." She left him to explore the large receiving room as she fetched the party requested.

The room's focal point was the grand pianoforte in the corner. He knew the Schuylers were well off, but he had no idea they were *that* wealthy. The walls boasted a few portraits of pleasant-looking young people, no doubt some of the Schuyler children, as they bore a resemblance to the Major General.

Elizabeth's breath caught as she entered and spied Alexander perusing the artwork. He was simply beautiful. She hated the term—he was a *man* after all—but God, he was beautiful. Smooth, flawless skin, dark auburn hair, eyes so blue they were at once piercing and warm. Her silly friends had mentioned his impressive looks and demeanor in giggling conversation, but they had no idea how striking a figure he cut in person.

"Mister Hamilton?"

Alexander turned slowly on his heel and met Elizabeth's eyes as she glided across the room to clasp his hands. He'd briefly wondered if seeing her here in the daylight and in simple clothing would diminish the intensity of his feelings. It did not. "Elizabeth, you are breathtaking," he intoned.

She smiled up at him. "I'm so pleased you called. Our parting last week was…abrupt." Elizabeth blushed as the circumstances of their parting—and their meeting—flooded her mind. She glanced away, embarrassed.

"Look at me." Her eyes again met his, their hands still clasped. "I could not stay away. I had to know you were not a heady dream following too much wine. I had to see you, perhaps touch you, to believe you are real," Alexander murmured in a low voice.

"Not here," she warned. "I want you to touch me, and I want to touch you, but this is neither the place nor the time. We have no privacy here." She paused, her eyes searching his face for an alternative.

It was true. The noise from the other rooms was unwavering and occasional passing footsteps outside the door were a reminder that they were not alone in the house.

"Would you meet me at my rooms? It is not an impressive space but it is quiet and private," he suggested, half expecting her to laugh in his face.

She studied his face a moment longer before briefly averting her eyes. Then, after seeming to resolve some unstated question in her mind, she once again met his gaze. "I should very much like that, sir."

Alexander paced around his room, reading the spines of all the books in his library. Elizabeth wasn't late. He was early. And eager. Maybe too eager. Something about this woman jolted his insides and left him feeling like a guileless school boy amid his first real crush.

He tried to relax in the chair the Livingstons had given him as a housewarming gift. It was luxurious, better than any he'd felt previously. He sank into it. Falling, drifting to that wonder-filled place near sleep.

Three short knocks sounded. He sprang to attention, soldier-like, and answered.

"Alexander. I-I didn't mean to wake you, sir." It was Elizabeth, stunning in an emerald satin gown trimmed with fine lace, and a string of pearls around her neck.

"Oh. No, Elizabeth." He ran his eyes up and down the wondrous shape that lay beneath the luxurious fabric. "My goodness. By all means, please, come in. You look…um…you look absolutely stunning tonight."

Elizabeth blushed and curtsied.

"Shall I join you, sir?"

"Yes, if it pleases you."

"It does."

She brushed past him, touching his thigh with her fingertips.

"Would you like something to drink?" Alexander asked.

"No, sir. I should very much like to sit down, if that is acceptable."

Alexander showed her to the sitting area of his meager rooms. She sat on the settee and looked up at his face. She now had taken off her lace neckerchief, revealing the gentle curve of her shoulders and the perfect pale skin of her throat.

"My God, Miss Elizabeth. You are positively ravishing."

"Do you like, sir? I wanted you to like me."

He was on her body then, gently at first, kissing her neck and shoulders, exploring each inch of wondrous flesh. His hungry mouth engulfed hers. She swooned beneath him with a murmur and moan.

They moved to his bed. She shimmied out of her gown as he positioned her hips below his. He caressed her neck, moving his way down her heaving chest. His ardent tongue swirled between her breasts before easing down her comely stomach. Once there, he kissed her navel with sweeping, whispery strokes, plunging his tongue playfully inside and out.

Then he did something Elizabeth had never experienced in all her years.

Alexander gently kissed the outer lips of her burgeoning wetness and then slid his warm tongue inside her. He found her protruding nub and began to excite her in earnest. At first, it was the strangest sensation she'd ever felt. His mouth on her like this, his tongue penetrating her again and again, but after a while, she began panting and lifted her hips to his face, inviting him deeper inside.

She met his searching tongue's every pass with a lunge of her own, while she, now sopping wet with desire, found she wanted more. What had begun as a delicate tickling within was replaced by a most exigent need to have him put his manhood inside her. And now.

Alexander noticed her need and momentarily stood by the bedside. He hurriedly pulled down his trousers and tore his waistcoat off. He pressed himself against her.

"*Yes.* I want. *Yes,*" Elizabeth cooed as Alexander pushed himself in and out of her.

Yes, Alexander thought. *This is what it is supposed to feel like inside a woman. Warm. Inviting. Perfect…*

He quickened his tempo as Elizabeth's cries intensified. She came with a helpless groan; there were no words for what she felt, other than one amorphous *yes*. He came almost instantly after, a wave of euphoria covering his face. He settled to rest on top of her. Afraid his weight was now noticeable and an onus, he rolled off her, studying the ceiling, still brushing her heaving bosom with a playful finger.

"Miss Elizabeth, may I say…may…"

"You may say whatever you want, sir."

"May I say that was amazing?"

"Alexander, surely, you jest with a young girl."

He then playfully pulled away.

"No. I do not jest. I feel…"

"And just what is it you feel, then?"

"I'm not sure yet."

"Please don't tease me."

"I'm not. I would not."

"Please, then."

"I think we should definitely see each other again. If you like."

"I would like. I would like that very much, Mr. Hamilton. Kitty would like it, too. The three of us."

"Really?"

Elizabeth blushed then, embarrassed and enamored, simultaneously. She turned away from him and stared at the painting on the far wall.

Alexander smiled. Was this going where he thought it was going? Two women at one time? The thought aroused him beyond comprehension; the guileless boy was about to come of age in a way he'd never dreamed of.

Alexander made his way through the streets of Elizabethtown. Lectures today had been unremarkable, though he was admittedly distracted by thoughts of Kitty and Lizzy, Lizzy and Kitty — both of them — alone and together. Repeatedly throughout the day, he forced his thoughts back to his studies. *Get your head together,* he ordered himself.

Footsteps sounded beside him, and he glanced to his left to find Kitty. She seamlessly slipped her arm through his and they continued to walk down the street together without missing a step.

"Good afternoon, darling," Kitty greeted him in a low voice. "Is it not perfect right now? It is cool and the sun is not oppressive in the least at this hour, is it?"

"It is not," agreed Alexander, "but it is not the sun I find so vexing of late. Thoughts of you and your dearest friend interfere with even my simplest cogitations." He smirked sideways at Kitty, though she saw through the façade, sensing his sincerity.

Kitty beamed up at him while they walked. "Perfect," she trilled, "because I am here to plan with you."

"Plan?"

"We are to execute the plan you made with Lizzy, are we not?" she inquired, a devious glint in her eye.

"Indeed," Alexander replied.

"First, you should know that the Schuyler Mansion — the Pastures — is a very old place, one of the first grand homes built on this continent," Kitty began.

"It was very grand," Alexander agreed. "But what has this to do with our surreptitious and sensuous plans?"

"Will you please allow me to speak?" Kitty retorted, jokingly vexed. She continued, "It is very old and there are places — corridors and whole rooms — unseeable from the outside. Indeed, most of those on the inside do not know of their existence, family included."

"How can this be? With so many children, some must have stumbled upon it."

"That is precisely what I thought, but I have seen them and I assure you, they are well hidden. Only Lizzy and her eldest sister, Angelica, know of it. Ages ago, when they were only girls, they cared for their ailing grandfather. He spoke of hidden corridors and a private room."

"The clichés are toppling over each other, you realize, darling." Alexander was incredulous. They crossed the street and continued past markets and shops.

"Allow me to finish. After he died, Lizzy and Angelica searched for the hidden entrance and lo, they found the thing! The main room is quite splendid and they surmise their grandfather used it as a private place for quiet and escape, a place for contemplation and secret trysts. I suppose for the same things we hope to enjoy."

They stopped outside the entrance to Alexander's house. Kitty turned toward him and studied his face in the afternoon light. "To-morrow evening, Major General and Mrs. Schuyler plan to host a large party with many guests. It is some sort of concert, I believe; they do so quite often. Everyone will be quite distracted." She paused. "Will you meet us?"

Alexander entered through the gate Kitty had told him about.

The door slipped open, and she met him there with an enormous kiss. He flushed for some reason and tried to hide it by taking her hand. She led him down a dark corridor toward yet another room. Shafts of light shot out from beneath the door, and he heard music, good music.

They entered.

Elizabeth's secret chamber was immense, a cathedral of candlelight and shadow. An ornate chandelier glistened above a large silken bed in the middle of the room. Alexander noticed there were two stories. A slender staircase sat almost hidden to his left.

Damn, if the old man wasn't just telling his grandchildren a wild tale, he mused. *This room has seen things, furtive things, things not accepted in polite society.*

Handel's "Violin Sonata No. 6" trilled and made itself known in the background. Clearly, in some distant corner of the grand home, party goers reveled in a performance by a fine (doubtless European) virtuoso.

Kitty spoke first. "So, what do you think? Amazing, isn't it?"

"Yes. The Sonata is quite good. But, amazing? I much prefer his 'Fugue in G major.' I've told you so."

"Oh, you and your dirges. Bah. I meant the room…"

They both resurveyed the quarters.

"Yes. Quite impressive."

"I thought you would enjoy it. It's got everything. Wine, women, and song, as it were."

"And Elizabeth?" Alexander's heart leapt as the words left his mouth. Kitty shot him her patented wicked grin.

"Oh, she's here, of course. She's getting ready."

Getting ready. Splendid. Two of the most beautiful words ever uttered, thought Alexander.

He breathed in the sheer opulence before him. It was the richest amalgam of sex and sophistication he'd ever encountered. Of course, he'd seen countless paintings in museums and read about this type of thing in books. But this was real. Even better, this was corporeal, he thought. He could experience it with his extended fingertips, breathe in and savor its essence, and maybe even — one day — receive it into his heart.

He then felt a sudden, dull tug at his waistcoat. It was Kitty. Her mouth was moving, but no sound seemed to emerge from it. She gestured wildly with her arms. "Hello…? Anybody in there?" Kitty knocked him on the forehead with a gentle palm and smiled impishly. "I said, we should uncork the wine, you deaf mute."

"Yes, of course."

They moved toward the bar in the back of the room. An inordinately expensive Bordeaux sat atop a silver serving tray, three glasses surrounding it. Alexander fumbled with the cork. There seemed to be extra wax and string about it that prevented him getting the cork to rise. Kitty laughed merrily.

"Have you never opened a bottle? A fine one, I mean? Ha! Not to worry. Here, I'll fetch us something." Kitty leapt toward the stairs and ascended.

Alexander watched as she disappeared into the tenebrous shadows above. He continued to fiddle with the wine bottle, finally clearing the last of the extraneous wax and managed to cleanly uncork it. All smiles, he poured the Bordeaux into the three glasses, inhaling its redolent balm.

"Alexander. Thank you for coming. It is so good to see you." Elizabeth's voice was clear in the room as she descended the staircase.

Alexander suddenly looked up. He stood stupefied at the sight of her.

She was wearing a simple, beautiful gown, and with every step down he could see more and more of each lithe, perfect leg. She was even more stunning than when he'd first met her. His brain scrambled; her beauty was beyond his comprehension. Had he known this beauty before, had this beauty been beneath him as he partook of her willing perfection? And would she still want him now, he asked himself uncertainly.

Elizabeth approached Alexander. She was hoping to start quickly, but sensed a strange uneasiness about him. She slowed her walk and kissed him gently on the lips. He seemed to calm a bit at this and offered her a glass of wine. They sipped for a bit as the music continued behind them.

"Dance, my lady?" Alexander offered.

Elizabeth curtsied. "I would love to, sir."

They drew close and gently twirled to the muted tones in the distance. Alexander looked into Elizabeth's eyes. He drew her close and kissed her deeply, placing one hand on her hip, the other on her lower back. She responded in kind, even going so far as to place a gentle hand on his behind. They continued on, enjoying each other, holding each other tightly.

Then the music suddenly stopped.

They looked at each other, laughed for a second, and continued on without skipping an imaginary beat. Alexander even playfully put his hand on the small of her back and they engaged in a minuet for a few seconds before slipping back to their slow dance reverie.

Kitty descended the stairs, a different corkscrew in hand. She watched as they danced in silence, amazed that they didn't seem to notice the absence of music as they undulated in a singular motion, but she was even more amazed by the fact that they didn't notice as she brushed by them and settled herself at the bar.

Alexander kissed Elizabeth again, their tongues seemingly sated with every flick, but always going back for more.

Kitty paused as she poured another glass and watched them.

God bless them as they fall in love. These are two people I love, and I love that they are falling for each other. But, where is my love? Or more specifically, My Love? When I fall for someone, it will have to be at least as brilliant as this. It is fate, then. A book and bed sound good about now.

With that, Catherine retrieved her reticule and silently downed the last of Elizabeth's Bordeaux. She then smiled again at her would-be paramours and took her leave.

Elizabeth gazed at Alexander. He seemed distant. She touched his cheek.

"What are you thinking?"

"I'm not sure. Such a whirlwind of thoughts."

"Please. I'm sure my whirlwind matches yours. Most likely exceeds it."

"I came here wanting one thing. But then…but then…and I don't know that one thing could not still be something I want. But, no. Not now. I think."

"Alexander, you talk in riddles."

"I think I am falling in love with you, madam."

Elizabeth's cheeks turned rose red as she turned from him.

"Do you not feel even remotely the same, Elizabeth? If you don't, I will understand."

She bolted back toward him.

"Sir. I most ardently understand." With this, Elizabeth's cheeks turned a tad crimson. She then steeled herself. "I have felt the same since our eyes first met. I only ask that you be true with what you say."

"I speak truth, my love. Verily."

Elizabeth crushed Alexander with a hug, both arms tight along his spine. He responded with a soft kiss on her lips and moved down to her neck. Both sighed, feeling the complete rush of everything they were then, not knowing what might come.

Historical Note: Hardly a month after their courtship began, twenty-five-year-old Alexander Hamilton and twenty-two-year-old Elizabeth Schuyler decided to marry. The happy bride was described as, "beautiful, accomplished, talented, and well-born. Her vivacity, intelligence, and amiability had rendered her a universal favorite in the polished circles of Albany, at that time one of the most select and cultivated towns in the country."[1]

Following their marriage, Elizabeth typically seems to have become a historical footnote. Nevertheless, she was exceptionally active in her husband's social and political life, though she opted to work behind the scenes. For fifty years following Alexander's tragic and untimely death, Elizabeth upheld Hamilton's legacy. Theirs was a true love story fraught with compelling characters and intense sexual undertones, and the best parts are not fiction.

1. Samuel M. Smucker, *The Life and Times of Alexander Hamilton* (Philadelphia: G.G. Evans, 1858)

A BOSTON MARRIAGE

BY LINDA CUNNINGHAM

Our dear, fair city of Boston had become garrison to an indeterminate number of British troops who were meant to enforce the king's will and taxes upon the colonies. There was no care in Europe about the souls who might people these colonies, be they Tory or Continental sympathizers. The New World was seen only as a cache from which to garner raw materials and monies in order to fund senseless wars upon the Continent. If England bled us dry, it was of no concern to the Redcoats. They considered our beautiful land a wilderness and her people, barbaric.

It had been nearly a year since our stalwart militia had met the Redcoats at the bridge in Concord and now it had escalated to full warfare. Our brave patriots had laid siege to their own homes and fair surrounds with the ultimate plan of driving the occupying British troops back out to sea.

As a result of this siege, many secret plans were exchanged as patriot families saw the wisdom of evacuating the city. I had been recently affianced to my darling love, George Hancock, the son of a close friend of my dear papa. George had purchased a hundred acres of good farmland from a wealthy landowner in the town of Lunenberg some ways outside the city. He had begun construction on the house that would become our home, but our plans to wed were soon forced into postponement when General Washington asked

Mr. Henry Knox, a local bookseller, to travel to Fort Ticonderoga and return with the cannon and arms captured earlier that year by Ethan Allen and his Green Mountain Boys. Secretly, Mr. Knox had pressed every able-bodied man he could find into accompanying him on this venture, which, he said, would be the final undoing of the British occupation. My father, a staunch ally of General Washington, agreed to go, and my darling George accompanied him. My mother being dead many years, I was now alone in an occupied city.

There were other women living the same life, as well. The British took little heed of us, but we kept mostly indoors, frugally rationing our meager stores and hoping the siege would be successful before food ran out. In order to entertain ourselves, we often met together at a neighbor's house and enjoyed afternoons of sewing and talking. Sometimes one of us would be able to get our hands on some contraband tea or coffee, and those evenings were especially fine. However, this new habit was soon to change.

One such evening in late January of 1776, as the chill fog swirled into the city from the bay, there was a particularly large gathering in the house of Eleanor Smith. We were all crowded around the fire in her parlor, and as I looked round, there were many faces I didn't recognize. Something was happening. Eleanor stood up. "My dear ladies," she said softly, "I have news that is good news, but which may bring temporary hardship." There was a soft murmur throughout the room as the ladies tried to guess amongst themselves what the news would be.

One person finally spoke up. "Tell us, please, Eleanor."

Eleanor held her hands up until their curiosity overcame them and the ladies became silent. Then she began to speak. "I must impress upon you the urgency in which my news must be undertaken and the confidentiality with which it must be carried out. Intelligence received by our dear friend, Mrs. Margaret Gage, has revealed that our determined militia is persevering and that the cannon, now under the auspices of Mr. Henry Knox, moves closer to Boston with each day. The cannon will be placed around the city limits and the British will have no option but to evacuate by sea. Mrs. Gage has imparted to me that her sources urge every one of us to gather our children, servants, and necessary belongings; secure our homes; and make haste out of the city as soon as we can. Hopefully, most of you have relatives and acquaintances with whom you may make a temporary home until Boston is freed from the clutches of the British invaders."

She stopped and took a deep breath. "In the event that you do not, there are many colonial sympathizers along the route who have graciously volunteered to take people in. I have their names and will see you individually before you leave this house to give you the necessary letters of introduction. Thank you all, ladies." She then walked over to a desk at the far side of the room and began to sort through a pile of papers, leaving the rest of us to converse in wonder and no small amount of anxiety, amongst ourselves.

A panic seized me. Where would I go? I had no living relatives except Papa. I was not yet married. My George's family had long since evacuated, and I knew not where they were located. I had no wish to be left behind in a city full of surly British soldiers. Resolutely, I squared my shoulders and started toward Mrs. Smith to ask her help. I could only hope the British troops would soon be gone and George and I would be reunited.

Suddenly, I felt a light touch on my shoulder. Turning around, I faced a smiling young woman.

"Would you be Miss Mercy Hardon?" she asked.

"Why, yes," I replied, "I am Mercy Hardon. With whom do I have the pleasure of speaking?"

She had a fair, pleasant face and a comely, if generous, form. She was well-dressed and seemed close to my own age. She smiled more broadly than before and took my hand in her own gloved one. "I am Mrs. Patience Thomas," she said. "I am not very long married to Mr. John Thomas, who serves our colonial militia in this barricade of our occupied city. I am also the daughter of Aaron Parr, the man who sold your betrothed the land in our town of Lunenberg, to the west. We lately received word from George Hancock, advising us of your predicament and prevailing upon my dear father to afford you shelter until you may be rejoined with your affianced. Since my husband is serving here, I myself volunteered to come to escort you back to our home, where you are most welcome to stay."

"Can this be true?" said I, completely overcome with emotion and relief.

"Yes, yes, my dear," said my new benefactress. "After all, we will be neighbors after you wed and move to your new home. I must admit, however, I came hoping that in addition to fetching you, a visit to the camps outside the city on the return trip might allow me the good fortune to find my husband for a short visit."

"This is indeed more than I could have hoped for," I exclaimed, charmed by her easy nature and friendly smile.

"Well, then, let us be off to your house. Pack a trunk with your essentials. Do not trouble yourself should you forget anything. We have all the amenities you could desire at home. Our man Charles will call for you at six o'clock tomorrow morning. Please be punctual. We have bribed the sentries with whiskey and bacon, but we must not tarry."

"Where will you stay the night?" I asked. "You are more than welcome in our home."

Mrs. Patience Thomas leaned into me then with a giddy giggle. "I shall meet my dear husband this night and stay with him, wherever he is encamped, as a proper wife should do." Then she leaned closer and whispered in my ear. "However, may I say that my conjugal eagerness may goad me to exceed what is asked of a proper wife!" She burst forth with a laugh so gay and hearty that all heads turned toward her. I was somewhat puzzled by her remark, failing to grasp the appropriate meaning, but I laughed along with her for the sake of politeness.

Almost before I was aware, I was wrapped in my winter cloak with a heavy carriage blanket over my lap, sitting in the cushioned seat of a comfortable sleigh pulled by a stout gray mare, my trunk secured in the back. Mrs. Thomas sat beside me and held my hand. A nod from her to the grizzled man on the driver's box had us on our way.

The trip took most of the day, although the roads were clean and clear of drifts and potholes. We stopped three times to rest the mare and refresh ourselves at wayside inns and public houses. Mrs. Thomas was indeed a merry companion and brought me out of my self-doubt and insecurity with jolly stories of friends and family and life in Lunenberg, and how I would most assuredly come to love living there. It was nearing dusk as we approached a large white two-story house with four chimneys.

"What a beautiful home," I remarked.

"I fear we are a meager household at the moment," she said. "There is only Mama; Pearl, the housemaid; Anna, the cook, who is also Charles's wife; and myself. We are missing our men, I tell you! My father, my husband, and my brother are all serving in the militia."

"You have no children?" I asked.

"Oh," she laughed, "I have only been married since August, but we are hoping that children will begin to come along as soon as we are together without interruption. In the meantime, I may say that we will have fun in our pursuit of them! I am so happy to have you here. We will become fast friends! And from this moment on, you must call me Patience, for I shall call you Mercy." She laughed her hearty laugh and graced my cheek with a firm, welcoming kiss.

From the very beginning, I was welcomed with open arms by the whole household. Patience's mother, Mrs. Bancroft, was a plump, jolly woman who adored eating, and despite the call for stores to nourish our militia, there always seemed to be more than enough to eat at every meal. The housemaid, Pearl, was an agreeable young woman with a bright smile. Anna, the cook, was also housekeeper and a most talented player at whist, in which we indulged nearly every evening after our meal. Only Anna's husband, Charles, seemed taciturn, but he was nonetheless light of nature and merely engrossed in his daily work. This was our little household during the winter that our new nation was taking shape.

One evening, Patience and I were sitting up later than was usual. We were loath to leave the fire, as it was particularly cold that night. Charles came in and informed us that although he had lit the fire in Patience's room, the flue in the fireplace in my own chamber, he regretfully informed us, seemed clogged and had smoked dreadfully.

"Oh, this is indeed terrible!" Patience exclaimed, drawing her woolen shawl more closely around her shoulders. "You shall be frozen by morning!"

"I shall be fine," I assured her. "The coverlet is batten wool and very warm."

"I will not hear of you sleeping in there," she persisted. "You must sleep with me in my bed. We will be warm and it will be jolly fun as well. We can gossip till morning if we choose!"

So saying, she took my hand and pulled me out of my chair. "Come, let us go up to bed now. The whole household has gone to sleep!"

I followed her out of the room, hoping I would get some sleep amongst the chatter with which she would undoubtedly fill the night-time hours. Holding our tallow candle high, we tiptoed through the downstairs hall. As we passed the dining room, we both heard a soft rustling, and then a low, nearly indistinguishable moan. We halted in place and looked at each other. It was coming from the kitchen. Patience lifted her finger to her lips and bade me to follow. She proceeded through the dining room to the door that led to the kitchen. I, for one, was frightened. What if a renegade Redcoat had broken in and was ransacking the pantry? All that considered, I followed her in spite of it. Silently, she pushed the door open just enough so we could see into the room.

A dim glow washed the room. Two figures faced each other. One, a female, was seated on the heavy kitchen work table, the other, a man, stood very close to her. I strained my eyes to see more clearly and recognized Pearl. What was happening, I wondered. What was she doing with this man, and who was he?

I fixed my eyes upon the scene. I felt Patience's breath on my cheek as she, too, peeked into the dim tableau. As I watched, the man bent forward and kissed Pearl. George had kissed me twice, once on the cheek when he had asked me to become his wife, and once, quite quickly, on the lips, before he left with Mr. Knox. However, this was a kiss such as I had never witnessed, deep and slow. Pearl tipped her head back, and he kissed her on her throat. I heard a soft moan escape her lips. Then the man straightened and put his hands on her shoulders. I watched in disbelief and confusion as he slipped the bodice of her dress over her shoulders, exposing her corset. I gasped, but Patience pinched my arm. I was paralyzed with shock as I saw his hands reach down into her corset and free her breasts. It was not so dark that I could not see the nipples, erect and pink, nor the smile on the man's face as he pulled and pinched them playfully. An unfamiliar feeling, almost a swoon, washed over me as he lowered his lips to them and kissed each one in turn.

I felt Patience pull on my arm. In a daze, I followed her. We did not speak until we had climbed the stairs to her room and shut the door behind us. I stood, dumbfounded and trembling.

"Did you witness that!" Patience hissed in a stage whisper. "That is Samuel, our Deacon's son! As you can assume, he is very fond of our Pearl!"

"What was he doing with her! What will your mother say?" I was scandalized by what I had witnessed.

"Mother does not know! She's been asleep for hours."

"You will not tell her?"

Patience gazed upon me strangely. "Of course not," she said slowly. "Pearl seemed to be enjoying herself."

I did not know how to reply to this, so I said nothing. My senses were beginning to return, and I could feel the warmth of the fire in the grate. Patience was beginning to get undressed. "Let's get into bed!" she said. She disappeared behind a screen and emerged a minute later clad in a white cotton gown trimmed with lace. For the first time I was aware of her ample bosom and plump backside. She washed her face quickly in the basin. "Hurry," she hissed at me. I followed suit, washing my face and undressing behind the screen. I pulled my cotton gown over my head and scrambled into the bed beside her. We lay in silence for a while, our loosed hair spreading on the pillows.

Finally, Patience said, "Oh, Mercy, I do miss my husband so! He would touch me just so! Just as Samuel was touching Pearl! I so envy them their mutual caresses. It has made me yearn for John in my loins! Do not you miss the kisses of your George?"

I felt my face grow hot and was glad for the dim light of the candle. There had never been talk of loins in my home. "I—I—well… George has kissed me but twice," I confessed. "It is not proper until after marriage."

Patience raised herself on her elbow. "Surely he has kissed you more than that? Has he not touched you? Touched you as a lover?"

At this remark, I was so shocked that I could say nothing, but only shook my head.

Patience stared at me. In a serious voice, so rare for her ebullient self, she said, "Why, John and I knew each other so well, we could hardly wait to be married just to finish what we had started! We could not keep our hands from each other. Are you not afraid of becoming a wife with so little knowledge of what it means?"

I could not lie to her. She had become a dear and trusted friend. I allowed myself the privilege of a confession. I nearly choked back tears, my emotions were so high. "Yes, it is true. I think I am afraid of what a wife must do at the bidding of her husband. When George has kissed me or held my hand, I have felt odd and giddy, yet I know not what should follow or what may happen on the night we must occupy the same bed. I am afraid to fail as a wife! I have heard whispers and rumors of pain and that men entirely change their character when called upon to—to—to perform their duties as husbands. What am I to do?"

Patience sat up in the bed and took both my hands in hers. "Oh, my poor, poor dear little friend! You have had nobody to talk to, no friend to tell you of the ecstasy that awaits! I know of some women who are not so fortunate and their husbands are not loving, but for me and many of my peers, being in the marriage bed is the most wonderful experience! We giggle about it amongst ourselves, and often! In the city, folks are so staid and prim. Here in the countryside, we enjoy ourselves! My heart beats hard this moment with the longing for it! I shall tell you how it is. It is transporting. It is magical. It is the jolliest fun two people can have together!"

She lay back down, and drew me close in her arms. "You must not fear, dear friend. George as you describe him appears to be a loving and affectionate man and he will no doubt treat you to delights you cannot imagine! Lie here with me and ease your mind. You may ask me any question and I promise you I will tell you the truth."

"Thank you, my dearest," I whispered. "You are such a comfort to me." I sighed contentedly and pressed against her warm form while she most delicately stroked my arm in a comforting fashion.

I was nearly asleep, my mind lulled by her gentle touch, when her strokes became longer, skimming my whole arm. I felt her fingertips caress my forehead, next to my hairline and follow the curve of my cheek to the hollow of my throat. The gentle tickle felt lovely and warmed me.

"You are very fair," Patience whispered into my hair. "Any man would be proud to become your husband. Your countenance is beauty personified." Her fingers were playing in the dip between my breasts and a slow, tingling sensation awakened in my nipples. Unbidden, I felt them grow hard and taut. Patience spread her hand flat and drew it slowly over my breast. Through the sheer cotton, I could feel my nipple straining. She gave a little chuckle. "These are the caresses my husband gives me," she whispered, "and you see, you are responding as though I was making love to you. These are the touches you and George shall give each other." She kissed me very lightly on the lips. Her mouth was sweet and soft. "You have nothing to fear! You will not fail as a wife." She grew bolder, saying, "Here, I shall show you more."

I was powerless to oppose her. I was so warm and at ease, and her touch was so soothing. So comforted was I, I lifted my face and kissed her cheek. Now her hand focused on my breast. Her fingers plucked at the nipple through the soft cloth. Slowly, she rolled me away from her and onto my back. Leaning on one elbow, she used her free hand to explore both breasts now, squeezing gently until I felt myself moving to meet her touch.

I felt her move and opened my eyes. She knelt above me, smiling. "I would deign to see you as George will see you," she said. I made no reply, mesmerized as I was. "I will lift your shimmy." I nearly lost my breath as she gently rolled up the garment around me, but I made no move to stop her. I soon found myself exposed and naked from my breasts to my toes. An unfamiliar, yet pleasant sensation started between my legs and crept up into my belly. My heart beat faster. My breath came in little gasps.

"You are a beauty!" she said happily, pinching my nipples. "Such lovely breasts, full, with nipples so pink and ripe, I might eat them!" So saying, she bent her head and sucked at each one, gently pulling at them with her teeth. A moan escaped me, and my hips moved involuntarily. Now her hands traveled down my belly. She bent and kissed my navel, allowing her tongue to penetrate and rim it with tiny licks. My face felt feverish and hot. I clamped my legs together with the tension.

"And here," said Patience, up on her knees, "here is the prize." She ran her fingers through the hair that grew, curly and thick, between my thighs. "So lovely. So sweet." She bent her head and buried a kiss in the hair. I groaned. The feelings were overwhelming and wonderful, frightening and confusing, addicting and maddening. My hips moved again.

"This is where your husband will want to be." Her hands were on my thighs, stroking and squeezing. "You will open your lovely legs for me and I will show you who you are and from whence these feelings originate. Will you do that for Patience?"

"Please," I gasped.

She parted my legs with the utmost tenderness. Wider, and wider still, until I lay open and ready for something I knew not but yearned to have. I opened my eyes, which had been clenched closed. Patience smiled at me and drew her gown off over her head. She was beautiful, kneeling there between my legs. Her breasts were large, her waist small and tight, her hips curved out to form plump thighs. I felt myself yearning to touch her. I reached up and touched her nipple with my fingers.

"Aha!" She laughed. "You are beginning to understand. Yet be patient, my dear student. There is more to learn first." Softly, she ran her hands up my thighs until she cupped the center of my emotion between them. Bending her head, she lowered her lips to the spot. Gently she eased her tongue between the folds. Instantly, every nerve in my body was alive with the most wonderful sensation. She began to lap, slowly at first, pushing, prodding, titillating me with delicate little sucks. I raised my hips to her face. She was licking me fiercely now. My body felt white hot.

Raising her head, she whispered, "You are most sweet." With the most delicate of touches, her soft fingers spread the lips of my passion. "This is your cunny," she said. "Some also call it 'twat' or 'cunt.' It is the center of delight for you and within it lies the spot which will send you to heaven and back." Her fingers began to stroke between the lips. I felt my own wetness dampening my skin. Carefully, slowly, Patience pushed and stroked alternately until one finger slipped into that place never before entered. A small squeal escaped my lips. She pushed the finger in deeper and with the other hand, squeezed and rubbed the hard little knob that lay hidden in the lips of my cunny until it swelled and throbbed. Now she began to work her finger in and out, rubbing all the while. I twisted and turned, moaned and gasped, until I felt I should be laid unconscious by the wave of passion that washed over me. No sensation I had previously felt could in any way compare. I felt my cunny, as Patience had instructed me to call it, clamping down on her finger, gripping, pulsing, as I seemed to float away in a crescendo of desire.

At last Patience collapsed by my side, breathing audibly. I lay still for a moment, trying to make sense out of the experience, but the warmth of her silken skin next to mine suddenly fueled a heretofore unknown wanton desire within me. I ventured to place my hand on her round hip and slide it across her soft belly. "I desire to touch you as well," I whispered in her ear.

Patience laughed merrily, and opening her legs, she took my hand and place it between them. "It would pleasure me to have you do so. Please, please explore. It has been so long since I have been touched thus." Her hips moved to better accommodate my hand and I allowed myself to give way to the new fierce feeling that possessed me. I raised up and parted the lips of her wet cunny with my fingers, as I had felt her do to me. The hot orifice was wet as well, and I bent my head to taste it. A salty sweetness filled my mouth, and I lapped at her with my tongue. Deeper I pushed my tongue into her, reveling in this new game we had discovered between us. My hand wandered all over her body. There was so much of her to explore, and I yearned to know every part of her. I put a finger into her, then another and another. I pushed in and out, watching the ecstasy form on her face. Suddenly, I was seized with a passion. I rolled her over and ran my hands over the white rounds of her ample buttocks.

"Oh," she cried. "Oh, dear! Oh, my! Mercy! Mercy! You make me weak." She moved her hips and her buttocks wiggled in a most adorable way. I squeezed them wantonly, then opened her legs wide so that I might kneel between them and play with those lovely orbs. I kissed them and gently bit them. I ran my finger down the crevice between them and was struck with the desire to part them and explore the sweet dampness there. I gripped her buttocks somewhat roughly and spread them. Again, she cried out, "Oh! Oh! Spread me! Yes! Yes!"

"Certainly every part of you is as beautiful as the next!" I replied, breathing in the sweet, musky scent of her most privy places. There was the intimate, private little orifice, puckered tight, and gently pulsing with desire. I lightly skimmed over it with my finger, playing round it, tickling it and pressing it. And there was the place that made her a woman, beckoning me. I sunk my fingers into her to the knuckles. With my other hand, I sought the longish, hardening ridge between the folds of curl-decorated skin. I squeezed and rubbed her, pumped my fingers in and out like a piston until at last she cried out, stiffening. She clamped down on my fingers, lifted her buttocks up and back, and tumbled over into the bedclothes.

Spent, satiated, and exhausted, we slept in each other's arms until morning.

After that, we played often at our games. Patience grew bolder with her lessons, awakening in me a desire that matched her own. One night, as we lay in her bed, she said, "Of course, my meager fingers cannot compare to the pleasure you will receive from your husband's cock."

"What is it like?" I asked, being very curious.

"Have you never seen one?"

"Never."

"Oh, my silly one," she giggled. "Well, I shall tell you about it. It hangs limp between the legs of a man until he is driven by amorous thoughts or touches. Then, the mighty cock springs into forward to the call for action, becoming erect and hard. It is quite long, about eight inches, and the man puts it into the woman's cunny with no little force, working it back and forth until he is spent and his seed is inside her."

"Does it hurt?"

"Oh, no, that is, even if it begins to hurt at the first go, or the first time a virgin such as yourself is entered, the sensation brought on by his mad thrusting soon replaces any sense of pain with the pure essence of pleasure. When John enters me, I feel it to the core of my gut and his motion leaves me hot and breathless."

I was beginning to feel a tingling between my legs again. "What else does he do?" I asked. "Will George do the same with me?"

"Oh, I feel no doubt but that he will," answered my friend. "John also enjoys entering me from behind. He will turn me on my stomach over a mound of pillows and come into me thus. In that way, he also plays with my arse." She giggled. "Sometimes he puts his finger in there, as you nearly did at our first session. You very much surprised me. You will be a passionate wife."

I felt the blush creeping into my face at the memory and the tingling between my legs grew stronger. "Oh my!" I gasped. "What does that feel like?"

"He rubs it first, and sometimes wets it with a little spit, so that it will allow him entry more easily. He is very gentle and once his finger is in, he moves it slowly around as he thrusts his cock in and out of me. I feel the fullness of passion everywhere, being stuffed in every orifice I have!" She laughed merrily and squeezed my breast. "You must try it."

"Does a man like to have his cock touched as well?"

Patience laughed again. "Oh, yes. And, more so, he likes to have his wife take it into her mouth and caress and suck it with her tongue!"

"Really! You make no jest?"

"I make no jest. John was a patient and kind teacher and had me practice first. He taught me by putting his finger in my mouth and guiding me. Here, I will show you, although my finger is not nearly as big as his, and a hard cock is bigger still. First, give me yours."

She lifted my hand to her mouth, and taking my index finger between her full lips, she sucked at it wantonly, moving her mouth up and down from knuckle to fingertip. "There," she said. "You have the motion. Now try to imitate it." She held up her finger and I took it into my mouth. "Suck as hard as you like. John told me he liked it when I suck very deeply. And it's important to relax the back of your throat so that the whole shaft might fit in at once, thereby heightening the man's pleasure. You must also, with your free hand, stroke and caress his ball sack, as this, too, adds to his enjoyment."

I sucked very hard, and as I did so, my passions increased. I wiggled closer to Patience. "You see," she continued in her professorial tone, "the more passion you impart on your husband, the more you must have for yourself!" She withdrew her finger and proceeded to make a pile of the pillows. "I will bring you to your climax in the way I described to you so that you will know the feelings that await you. Lie thus as I have told you." She pushed me gently over the pillows so that my naked buttocks were elevated and open to receive her every whim.

She parted my legs, kissing my cunny from underneath. "You are very wet," she said, "and this is good. It betokens the passionate nature lying within." Her tongue darted in and out of me. My blood thundered in my ears. Finally, she rose behind me and inserted her fingers. Where, due to nervousness, I was only able to take one finger in the beginning of her tutelage, I was now able to accommodate three very comfortably. She thrust them hard into me, to try to reproduce the motions of a man.

"Sometimes a playful spanking is fun," she said, and smacked me repeatedly quite hard on my buttocks.

I jumped at the first sting, but then the sting grew warm and the warmth grew hot. I spread my legs wider. With the fingers of her one hand still busy inside me, Patience began to explore my arsehole with her free hand. She sucked at her own fingers until they were wet and then wet them further in the juices that flowed from between my legs. Then she touched that tight orifice, tickling round it until I groaned and longed for her to enter. Finally, after teasing me until I felt I might die, she slowly worked the tip of her finger into me up to the first knuckle.

"Oh! Oh my! Yes! It is lovely! It is lovely!" I thought I would swoon as she began to roll it round and round inside me. I reached my climax and collapsed, exhausted. Patience laughed and lay down beside me.

"You see," she said, "there is no end to the fun you can have!"

There was not much snow that year and this made the time more lengthy and tiresome as we awaited any word at all about Mr. Henry Knox and his company with the cannon. Patience wanted so badly to break away, to take the trip into Boston, and meet with her dear John.

She had begged her mother more than once, but Mrs. Bancroft was firm in her denial. "It is no safe time to be abroad. Many wives have suffered the same as you, my dear. Myself included. Think you I do not miss your father, Mr. Bancroft? And a man of his age, camped out in bivouac in the dead of winter! Why, I worry every day till I am weak with it. The best and most honorable way we can serve them is to see that business is done here. Now, I will hear no more about it!"

After one such talking to, Patience sat glumly by fire in the parlor. I sat beside her and tried to be a comfort. "It is fortunate we have one another," I said. "We shall surely be rewarded when the British are routed and our men return." Very subdued, she nodded passively and leaned her head on my shoulder. Had we known the adventure that awaited us, we would surely have elected to continue our waiting, however tedious.

Our deliverance from boredom, along with our introduction to danger, came that very next day. It was late in the afternoon. The weather was particularly unpleasant, spitting a mix of rain and ice. The sun had set and the lamps were lit. It had been a particularly difficult day for everybody, for Charles had slipped on the icy steps of the kitchen entrance and very near crippled himself, pulling a muscle in his back. He could not stand up straight. Anna and Patience and I helped him into the house and laid him down in the little warm keeping room off the kitchen with a glass of whiskey to ease his pain. He had drifted off into a fitful half-sleep and we sat in the parlor close to the fire playing halfheartedly at whist. Suddenly, the dogs began to bark. Unaccustomed to such disturbances at this hour, we all looked up. A loud knocking came from the back door of the kitchen. This was very odd, since visitors invariably used the front door. Mrs. Bancroft held her fingers to her lips. She rose from the whist table, and opening a closet in the fireplace corner, she brought forth a musket, powder horn, and ramrod. We all sat silently while she loaded the flintlock and rammed the ball down the muzzle. Then she nodded to her daughter. We all followed her out to the kitchen. Again, the knocking was heard above the frantic barking of the dogs, who leaped and pawed at the door.

"Who is there?" Mrs. Bancroft called.

"Please, allow me entrance," came a male voice.

"Identify yourself," Mrs. Bancroft insisted, lowering the muzzle of the flintlock.

"I come from the company of Henry Knox," pleaded the voice, "with word from him and Messers Hardon and Hancock."

I forgot myself and the potential danger at hand and sprang forward, yanking open the door. A gust of wind blew snow and ice in around us as we faced the dark figure standing in the doorway.

"Enter, then," Mrs. Bancroft barked. "Explain yourself, and do not trifle with me." She leveled the rifle at the stranger, and he entered the room. He was a mere boy, wet to the skin and shivering.

"What news have you?" Mrs. Bancroft demanded.

"Have you word from my father? From Mr. George Hancock, as well?" I asked.

"I do," said the boy. "I bear extremely important messages for General Washington concerning the siege. Mr. Hancock gave me leave to stop here. He assured me I could find colonial sympathizers with food and dry clothing."

Mrs. Bancroft lowered the flintlock and said, in a kind voice, "Then come in. News of the cannon must be very important indeed. Anna, please get this young man something to eat. Make sure it is hot, and fetch some cider, as well. Come, come in and sit. Patience, go to the press in your brother's chamber. Methinks there are dry clothes there that would fit this young man. Mercy, take his coat and hang it by the fire to dry. Take care lest you singe it!"

We scurried to accomplish our tasks, eager to hear what the messenger had to say. Soon he was seated in front of the fire, in dry clothing, with a trencher of stew and a tankard of hot, hard cider. We crowded round him. Mrs. Bancroft, by virtue of her being the lady of the house, had learned the boy's name to be Tom Johnson and asked the important questions. "What is your news, then, Tom?"

The poor boy was very hungry and hardly paused in his meal as he answered. "The cannon are not so very far away, ma'am," he said. "I must get to the encampment outside Boston to tell General Washington that Mr. Knox means to swing them around to the Dorchester Heights. The General must know of this plan now. There is a problem, however." He stopped talking to stuff his mouth with stew and then continued. "Redcoats have managed to break through the siege lines at several points and they have commandeered several houses temporarily abandoned by their occupants who had need to flee. They range between the militia lines and the outside, looking for just such people as I, who may be attempting similar missions.

I must not be captured. The city of Boston is at stake. I shall need assistance getting through."

We were then startled by footsteps. Looking up, we saw Charles hobbling into the room. "Such a mission will be dangerous," he said. "I have a plan. I shall drive you in the dray. There is a compartment underneath where spare axles and spokes are kept. A boy of your size could surely fit in it and be hidden. I am an old, crippled man. I shall say I am a Tory, a loyalist on my way back into Boston after being accosted by militia to the west."

It was a good plan, save for the fact that Charles was hardly able to move. Mrs. Bancroft voiced what we all were harboring. "You would not make it two miles down the road in your condition, Charles! A good plan, but highly impractical at the moment."

Suddenly, Patience said, "Mama, Mercy and I are quite fit and healthy. We may drive the dray thus past the enemy with the same story for needing passage. We would have the advantage of being totally disregarded, being two young women."

My heart leaped. It was a daring plan. At first Mrs. Bancroft was very much opposed, but as the boy Tom, as well as Charles, insisted, Boston's fate lay in the success of the mission. At last she relented and we refined our plans.

The next day found us wrapped in warm cloaks, driving east toward Boston. Tom, the messenger, was sealed in the compartment beneath the dray. He was safe, but we did have concerns for his physical comfort!

Sunset saw us approaching the city. It had been a very quiet journey thus far, although we were now quite hungry and a bit chilled.

"Are there any houses along the way?" I complained. "Perhaps they would give us something to eat."

"We dare not stop," Patience replied.

"Look!" I pointed ahead. A large white house, lights burning in the windows, lay ahead.

"We shall have to pass by." Patience was firm in her resolve, but passing by the place was not to be.

Just as we approached the house, two uniformed men bearing rifles stepped into the road. Redcoats!

"Stop, by order of the king!" one shouted.

Patience halted the gray mare and the men, rifles leveled, approached the dray, one to each side.

"Where do you go, in the middle of this cold night?" sneered the one closest to Patience.

"We must see to our grandmama, who is unable to travel to us. She is old and alone and waiting for us to come to tend her," Patience said with a coy smile.

The Redcoat eyed her suspiciously. "I cannot allow you passage without a search," he said. "Corporal, hand down these wenches. We will bring them to the Colonel."

Patience and I exchanged startled looks, but she nodded to me to comply with the soldiers. I took the hand that was offered to me and stepped out of the dray. We were escorted in to the house by the soldier who stopped us, while our dray was led away by the other. We could only hope Tom lay safe in his hiding place.

Once inside, we were led into a small dim parlor. "Sit," ordered the soldier, gesturing with his rifle. We sat primly on a narrow settee. "I shall ask the colonel to see you. He alone will decide what to do with you."

When he had left the room, Patience whispered into my ear. I could see she had been thinking.

"We must deter these men and allow Tom to escape the dray. Darkness will have fallen and should provide him cover. It is essential their attention be on us and not that which we might carry in the wagon. Are you prepared to do what you must for your country?"

"What do you mean?" I asked.

"We must do whatever we must to divert and hold the attention of these soldiers. We must use our minds, our sharp wits, and perhaps our bodies as well."

Now I understood. My stomach heaved at the thought, but I bravely nodded.

"Such a brave beauty you are," said my friend, kissing my cheek. "Now follow my lead."

The Redcoat returned shortly to the room. He no longer carried his rifle. "You will see the colonel now," he said brusquely, motioning us impatiently through the door. He herded us down a narrow hallway and then into a large, bright living room, well-warmed by a crackling fire. We could see now that our enemy escort was very tall and well-built with black hair and bright blue eyes — quite handsome.

"Sir, here are the wenches found on the road."

Seated at a writing desk at the far end of the room facing us, was a British colonel. He was somewhat portly, with graying hair, and not as tall as our younger escort. "Approach the desk," he ordered, with a small sneer of a smile. We did as commanded. "So, you are traveling to see your grandmama?"

"Yes, sir," Patience said.

"I do not believe it," the colonel said harshly. "I say you are spies, trying to go to the encampment."

"Oh dear!" I exclaimed. "Please do not think such nonsense of us! We do not even know where the encampment might be! We have no allegiance to the colonial militia."

"We are simply trying to go to our grandmama! We are only country girls on an errand," Patience added, feigning frustration and matching me lie for lie.

The colonel snorted through his nose. "I wonder," he muttered. He rose from his desk and came around to stand in front of us. "Pray, take off your cloaks."

"We have nothing hidden!" Patience insisted.

"I order you, to spare yourselves peril, take off your cloaks."

We slipped out of our outer clothes and stood waiting. The colonel circled us. At that moment, the other sentry returned and stood by his compatriot. Without taking his eyes from us, the colonel said to him, "Sentry, did you notice anything of interest or suspicion with the horse and cart?"

"I did not, sir."

"Corporal, secure all the entrances to this house and return at once."

"Yes, sir," answered the tall corporal. He left the room.

"I must interrogate you," said the colonel.

"Oh, please, sir," said Patience. "We must be getting along."

"Yes, I'm sure! Getting along to deliver intelligence straight into the hands of those who mean to undo the king!"

The tall corporal returned. "As ordered, sir," he said. He and the sentry stood on either side of the door.

I could contain myself no longer. I burst forth, "Sir, I can prove to you our loyalty to the crown! With a favor, more or less."

"A favor?" He arched his eyebrows. "What mean you?"

I exchanged a sidelong glance with Patience. "We have no money, sir, nor nothing of value. We are only country girls, but we are willing to share what we have."

"Am I to take that as it is implied?"

Patience took up the cause. She smiled. "We have been told by some that we are comely. In these dangerous times, there is a dearth of fun to be had. We propose a small party, here and now, for the benefit of you and your corporal and your sentry." She put her finger to her lips and lightly sucked at the tip, smiling all the while.

The colonel broke forth with a smile. "Well, then, a couple of country wenches willing to entertain the king's troops! A dalliance, men. Bring forth the whiskey. We shall celebrate the demise of Boston, which is soon to occur."

The sentry rubbed his hands together and rummaged behind some books on the shelf, bringing forth an earthenware jug. The corporal put out some small mugs and the sentry poured the whiskey into them and handed them round.

"Have you tasted whiskey before?" asked the colonel, taking a large swallow.

"Oh, dear, no," Patience simpered. "It is quite forbidden."

I giggled and lifted the mug to my lips. I sipped and swallowed. The liquid burned down my throat in a very pleasant manner. Patience followed my example.

"I propose a toast to this little soirée," the colonel said, lifting his tankard.

We all followed suit. The sentry was eying Patience hungrily. He also was tall and quite comely, with light brown curls falling to his shoulders and large brown eyes.

"Before you think us fools," the colonel said, "I must tell you, in order to preserve my reputation as an officer, I must order you searched. You could have something hidden beneath your petticoats."

Our plan had begun in earnest. I wondered if I could go on with it, my blood so thundered in my ears. I took another drink of the whiskey to fortify my courage.

Patience took a step closer to the colonel. "Why, Colonel, I invite you to see for yourself, in front of witnesses. I have nothing to hide. I will not interfere. Please, go forward with your search."

Patience held up her hands. The colonel loosed his cravat. "Very well." He took the fabric of Patience's skirts and lifted them up, exposing her voluminous petticoats.

"Sentry, assist me," he said. The sentry strode forth and took up the burden. The colonel continued his search, lifting the petticoats. Now Patience was exposed to her drawers. I stood, scarcely breathing, as he reached a beefy hand between her legs.

"Oh! Oh my dear Colonel!" gasped Patience.

The colonel laughed heartily. "I say, Sentry, I feel nothing hidden there, but would you deign to check as well?"

The sentry heaved Patience's skirts over one arm and bent her forward into the arms of the colonel who supported her. He reached through the slit in her drawers, feeling her buttocks.

"A twat is all I feel, Colonel," he said. "And a wet one, at that!"

"Some assistance from you," the colonel called, looking at me. I stepped forward. "Take down her drawers and be quick about it."

I lowered Patience's drawers, setting free her ample bottom for all to see. The colonel now bent Patience forward over the sofa and came round to stand behind her. A large bulge in his breeches confirmed that which I suspected. He unbuttoned the flap of his breeches and his cock sprang forward. It was the first one I had seen and I nearly swooned. It was not so long as it was thick and turgid.

"Each of you take a leg," he grunted, pulling up his shirt. The sentry and the corporal rushed forward, each taking one of Patience's legs. They lifted them up and parted them. Patience moaned. The colonel ran his hands over her buttocks, down between her legs to squeeze her cunny. He advanced. I stood as one hypnotized, watching as he thrust his cock to her, trying to gain entrance. His generous belly slapped against her bottom. He fumbled to find her cunny and sink his cock there. An idea then occurred to me.

"Let me help you," I proffered, and stepping to his side, I took his cock in my hands and guided it directly to its target. He groaned as it sunk to the hilt, and he began to thrust. The sentry and the corporal rocked Patience up and down upon the shaft. She gasped and called out in her ecstasy.

"Yes! Fuck as hard as you will! Fuck me!" she cried.

The colonel, complicit with her wishes, bucked over her harder and harder until at last she squealed and grew limp. The colonel's eyes rolled back into his head. He gave an enormous gasp and fell forward upon her, his breath heaving with the wonderful exertion.

Our soirée came to full fruition. I cast off my outer clothing with the help of the handsome corporal, who I found to be quite gentle and accommodating. I daren't tell him it would be the first time I felt a man's cock within me, but my heart palpitated with anticipation. All the men had shed their breeches. While Patience lay, entirely stripped, on the sofa between the sentry and the colonel, the corporal wadded up his clothing and bade me lay out on the carpet in front of the fire. I complied and he put the makeshift pillow under my head. Rolling up my shimmy, he bared my cunt, and after kissing me quite nicely, he bent his head to the prize.

I soon was transported by his tongue as it explored me inside and out. Heretofore, I had experienced only the caresses of Patience, but the corporal filled me with an even hotter desire, if that was possible. His tonguing was a bit rougher, a bit more invading. He inserted a finger into me and I cried out passionately. I twisted and turned as he thrust it in and out. Before I was quite aware, he was kneeling over me and I was looking straight at his rigid cock. It appeared so large to me, much longer than the colonel's, and a pleasing width. What would it feel like between my legs? Then I remembered what Patience had said. I raised myself to a sitting position and took his cock between my lips, hefting and squeezing his ball sack at the same time. I started slowly to suck and draw on it. He reacted exactly the way Patience had told of, groaning with pleasure, pushing it down my throat. I sucked until at last he withdrew. Thus lubricated, he opened my thighs and rammed quite violently into me. I gave a little shriek. There was an instant of some kind of pain, but the shock of the assault evaporated immediately in the face of the warmth and tingling that spread out across my entire body as he fucked me steadily. I was rocked to and fro by his forceful thrusts, and my cunny grew so hot I thought I should swoon away. Instead, the wash of my climax enveloped me as I felt him explode within me.

We lay thus and caught our breath. At last he rolled off me, laughing. "You are indeed a loyalist," he said with a chuckle.

The night continued as we turned our attention to the others. The colonel had recovered his energies and came up behind me. Circling my waist, he sat down on a chair and pulled me down on his lap. He hung both my legs over his own. "I hold a vixen here," he said. "Who would have her?"

Patience laughed and going down on her knees between my open legs, sucked awhile on my cunny. I writhed in passion. She entered me with her fingers, pumping at me until they were wet. The men hooted and howled with amusement. The sentry said, "I shall have some of that." Patience withdrew and he came into me. His cock was hard and the fucking was pleasing, but imagine our surprise when, as he withdrew to get a better angle, the colonel released me and grabbed the sentry's still stiff cock in his hand.

"I warrant I shall have some of you as well," he said, and he wrapped his lips around the sentry's member. The sentry's face showed momentary shock, but the pleasure of the sucking soon overcame any reservations he might have had, and he gave in to the feeling, thrusting it deeper into the colonel's mouth. We all clapped and huzzahed at this new folly, for we were silly with all the jolly times we were having. At last the colonel released him and impaled me upon his own cock. The sentry found the need to bury his pulsing cock deep within Patience who was held quite helpless in the arms of the corporal until the sentry spent himself.

This new wrinkle seemed to fire our blood. The fire had burned low, and it became nearly impossible to tell whose cock was buried in whom. The colonel even brought out his riding crop at one point and insisted upon spanking us all, then giving us each leave to whip him in turn. It was jolly fun. Finally, we collapsed together in a sweaty heap, exhausted, but immensely satisfied.

When Patience and I at last opened our eyes, the dawn had broke. "We have indeed succeeded," my friend whispered, squeezing my hand in victory.

We set out for home after a quick breakfast and a few friendly kisses from our companions of the night before. As the history books will surely tell, the British were routed from Boston by the cannon brought by Henry Knox and his company of patriots. We had succeeded in saving the city, as well as our loved ones, and the new nation in which we now reside was one step closer to becoming a reality.

Patience and I have remained fast friends and neighbors. When we are alone, we sometimes relive that bawdy night and, if truth be told, sometimes reenact parts of it to pleasure ourselves. We have never divulged to our husbands, acquaintances, or families how great a role our love for our physical liberties played in securing sweet liberty for all our countrymen.

M'LADY'S SECRET SERVICE

AS RENDERED VERBATIM
BY VIVIAN RIDER

To the editors: While cleaning out the personal effects of my recently deceased grandmother, I came across a small journal which contained the document below, copied in her own looping script. I believe that the journal and the document are from her days at Radcliffe as a research student of American History, because of a dated letter on faculty letterhead which I found pressed between its pages. The letter warned my grandmother of the repercussions that would come to her if she tried to bring this "spurious record" to the "sensationalist digests" of her youth, regardless of the strength of its "supposed veracity." I will always remember my grandmother — of agile mind to the end — as a lover of intrigues, tricks and deceptions, and the games of love and war. I sincerely believe it will be of great interest to your readers.

D irectress Abigail Adams,
This is my — Underagent Penelope Gooden-Plenny's — record regarding the operation at Trenton, on Christmas Day, 1776. I hope this correspondence arrives to you safely through our Sisters' usual channels of beguilement and inveiglement, that it finds you and your esteemed husband well, and that, not only has our Cause of Liberty been furthered beyond stopping, but that your very mandate which

has made such a zealot of me — the Empowerment of all Women in the New World — has also been secured.

I received my orders through a briefing from Agent Caty Greene and was presented with the written draft of orders which bore both your initials and those of General Washington. She was very discrete and notified me that I would be entirely at my own resources. While she tried to accompany her husband General Nathanial Greene throughout the campaign, she, her children, and the few domestics she had with her would be leaving for better shelter as the winter became as inhospitable as the war. But on the day I began my operation, as the weather turned for the worse, so it also favored the success of my mission.

In the late afternoon on the day of Christmas, I had met with that lecher, the nephew of Benjamin Franklin, Jemmy. As he and his loutish lads filled the wagon with the casked supplies for the operation and hitched the team of two horses, he chuckled and clucked to himself around his clay pipe while I tried to stay warm by the stable's stove. I was not wearing garments appropriate for either the weather or the war. Instead, I had the garb of a rich loyalist's housemaid, indeed one who should not be outside during a Christmas storm.

I embarked on my own and had to make several slow miles in the icy falling snow, which was getting heavier. At my best reconnoiter, it was late into the evening when I was about a quarter mile from the location of the action for my operation. I found a mile-marker half obscured in the snow off on the side of the road and ran my wagon into it. The right wheel collapsed under the impact. I put a carriage blanket around my shoulders, took two of the smaller casks from the wagon, and set out on foot.

I labored, walking in the snow, becoming quite wet and frigid, and soon saw the torches of the enemies' sentry. There were two Hessian corporals and their sergeant, which was fortuitous. I made plenty of noise as I approached, and wasn't alarmed when they pointed their muskets at me. Despite being encumbered with the small casks, I waved a silk handkerchief that was a small version of the Union Jack. They were still suspicious, but lowered their weapons. I spoke in broken German about the wagon of my loyal (but fictitious) employer, the broken wheel, and the many casks of ale in the back. I offered the small cask to the sergeant. He tapped a bit into a pewter mug that was in the shelter of the sentries' post, and his face lit up from its warmth after taking a draught. The American forces had disrupted their supply lines for the past week, and the wagon's load—on the holiday in particular—promised some comfort and folly.

Despite the fact that I had used only broken German, I am well-versed in the language, and knew from the orders he barked to the corporals that, so far, my ruse had worked. One bolted in the direction of the Hessians' encampment in Trenton, while the sergeant took my arm to help me through the now deepening snow. I made slow ladylike progress to purposefully stall, and soon the corporal was running in the other direction with three other soldiers, one of whom had the tools of a wheelwright. Things were proceeding nicely. I was led to the small house that Colonel Johann Rahl had occupied. The sergeant explained my predicament to the colonel better than I could. I knew Rahl had no command of English, but let the sergeant, who understood some, know what my offer for the night's shelter was: for the Hessians' hospitality I would repay them with the ale, if they could save my horses.

The colonel invited me in and pointed to the fire blazing in the hearth. He noticed how thoroughly soaked I was when I spread my sodden skirts in front of the fire—and I'm sure he noticed the shape of my body within, as it was illuminated from behind in this manner as well. He pointed to a small dressing room off to the side of the main room. Taking a tallow candle, I went into the room, leaving the door somewhat ajar. There were a variety of military uniforms and martial accessories with a dressing screen. I disrobed quickly, disregarding the modesty of the screen and not looking toward the door. I knew the colonel was watching me. I felt the warmth of the flickering candle caress my nudity, so frozen had I been. As all the clothes were men's, I chose a quilted, golden-colored, mid-length silk dressing jacket. I turned about in the candlelight so he could see me illuminated from every angle this time. By the time I emerged with the jacket on, the troops stationed outside had started to play Christmas hymns on a fife, squeezebox, drum, and fiddle. The ale had obviously arrived.

The colonel, standing at the mantle, firmly grasped his clay pipe which was between his teeth. Were it not for his teeth gripping the stem, I am sure his mouth would have been agape. Snapping from his reverie, he was about to call an officer to fetch him some of the ale, I assumed. I was not about to chance that he would have a drinking companion, and I quickly brought his attention to the one cask that the sergeant had carried for me from the sentries' post.

"Für Herr Colonel," I said, holding the small cask, implying that it was for him only. He tapped the distillation into a metal cup, and smelled it. I was an *eau-de-vie* distilled with the herb *damiana*, and I could smell its strong pungency from first tap. He balked at drinking it, so I took the cup from him, and drank deep, giggling as I did so. He finished the rest and, smiling, broke out two clean heavy glasses.

He drank deep in kind, and a sort of flush overcame him, and not from the fact he had his elbow upon the mantle, so close to the blazing fire. As he drank, I took stock of my enemy. He struck a true soldier's figure: broad and tall, though at present without wig and having a waistcoat open at the neck. His reddish hair was collected in the back with a black ribbon, and his moustache was heavily waxed in the Hessian fashion.

His forehead began to glow, as the *damiana's* aphrodisiac effect took over him. Nervously, he poured himself another glass, and looked quizzically at me. The solemn hymns from outside were slowly turning to a more jolly cadence, and there was some singing as the ale took its effect on the troops.

Even though I knew he had no knowledge of English, I began to thank him profusely in that way only a woman can talk to a man. The tongue of flirtation is unmistakable in any language. I laughed heartily and, to make my point, placed my hand against his chest. He looked down from his manly height — manly, but short of that of General Washington's. I half-closed my eyes and separated my lips, with my tongue slightly behind them in wait.

We kissed, long and hard. I loosely pulled at his bottom lip with my teeth. He gripped me by my shoulders, and I ran my hand inside his coat, stroking his chest. With my other hand I opened the dressing gown I had borrowed. His firm hand entered the jacket, and cupped each of my breasts, one at a time. I pushed my hands against his chest, and dropped my head backward, letting out a throaty sigh.

His head went inside the jacket, and the roughness of his moustache was a brilliant change from the smoothness of the silken jacket. After dragging his moustache across my nipple, he bit down on it, gently at first then harder. As he began to stoop down to kiss my belly, I firmly pushed back against his shoulders.

As he stood back upright, I went down to my knees and clawed at his breeches. I reached into the opening as far as I easily could and found that the *damiana* was working quite well. The German made a guttural lowing. I pulled his shirt from the waist of the breeches, and stroked his strong abdomen.

At last, the fall of his breeches yielded to my fingers. Out from them his pecker flew, stiff in the air like the mast of a ship. I reached in further to extricate his balls, as well. I massaged both with flitting hands and blew hot breaths across them in the chill night.

I wrapped my lips around the head of his cock, forcing more and more into my mouth, in hard drawn out movements, while working the shaft with pumps of my hand. His pelvis began to jut out, and his thighs shook quickly; they had become rigid. In fact his whole body had become as taut as his member in my mouth.

At this point there was a clear departure in the seasonal songs from outside, and the tunes took on a more bawdy turn, as was proved by the laughter and shouting from outside. The plan was working beautifully.

After several moments of this work, he wildly grabbed me underneath my arms and practically lifted me off the ground, as he led me over to a table. He spun me around and gently but firmly bent my upper body across it. He flipped the hem of the short dressing jacket up and caressed my buttocks for a moment the way a man may stroke a horse's flanks, and he prepared to mount me from behind.

I had heard that at the request that he build a defensive redoubt in Trenton, Rahl had dismissed it with the response, "Let them come; we will go at them with the bayonet." And so it was. With a forceful upward thrust he had entered me, feeling like a fiery iron compared to the chill I had been enduring just an hour before. His thrusts were accompanied by guttural noises, both of which were urged on by my lusty yells. I could see us both in the blurred silver mirror above the mantel—like heated and rutting felines in the flickering firelight.

While in this position, my mission had come back to me, but only briefly. I wondered where in the small house the official war documents might be. I used the moment and my vantage point to disguise my surveyance of the room by thrashing about on the table. But, as hard as I tried, I kept being overcome by the carnal revelry. My thrashing was genuine as I was being thrashed in kind.

He withdrew and stepped back from me to gain his breath and strip completely. He was breathing heavy and had broken into a sweat. His eyes were flashing, and the only thing drooping even slightly was his moustache, as the wax gave way. I spun around, still perched on the table, coyly crossed my legs, dropped the jacket completely off my shoulders — as its purpose for concealment was spurious any- way — opened my legs wide, and motioned to embrace him.

His step forward was forceful. He collided with me, entering me again. We more easily mated this time than his last penetration. Again I tried to keep my mission in mind, but so great was the lust we had conjured in the firelight, I was borne away with the moment.

His brutish thrusts increased in their intensity, and the sounds he made became growls. I could scarcely control my own voice, but knew our sounds would be drowned out by the racket the soldiers were making. It was the most wanton experience I have had to date. My Puritan parents, my minister father — they would be shamed up to the Gates of Heaven themselves, but none of this mattered as I was swept up in this tempest of animalism.

The colonel was getting unsteady on his legs, so overcome was he. I sensed it was his head that was swimming and not his stamina giving out. Still buried inside me, he grabbed me from the table, roughly clutching me by my buttocks, and moved toward a Savoy chair. He sat down with me atop him, and I instantly ground down upon him, so he filled me in the fullest deepness.

I ground my hips upon him, kissing his sweating forehead. I clutched his head to my chest, and his mouth found both my breasts. We remained like this for several moments, until I got an idea on how to best use the Savoy chair's construction.

I whirled about with my back toward him, and using the back of the chair for support of my hands and the short arms of it for one of my feet, I moved up and down in long, swift movements. The music outside had reached a feverish pitch, and I danced upon his cock to it. I could see us in that mirror as before, but I had never seen myself as such. The wildness and abandon — I was absolutely beautiful in my naked Jig of Nature.

The colonel was now breathing hard; his gasps seemed to have the Germanic accent. I knew he would not last long going on like this, but so heated was I, I never wanted to stop. I rose off him, and he looked absolutely worn, but I was not finished.

I pulled over a nearby velvet-covered hassock and worked my mouth around him again, to give him some period of rest. He was still quite rigid, so well did the distillate work. Taking my time, I beheld him in the firelight; a full handspan and a half of my own measure, and my fingers barely touched when I gripped the shaft. The sack of his balls hung low and full, so great was the heat we generated.

Sensing that my curiosity had been satisfied, he lifted me and spun me around again, laying me on my stomach across the hassock. He penetrated me almost from directly above. Clearly, from the fierceness of his thrusts, the fog that settled upon him had cleared. The pace and cadence of the music outside was reaching one furious peak after another, and as it rose and fell, with it I climaxed over and over again.

The moment's duration was timeless; I know not for how long we went like this. But, when the music stopped, or we simultaneously became aware of its ceasing, we both looked at each other—me craning my neck to see him—and laughed heartily. It was the same in any language.

The mission came back to mind, and while he still stood, I sat on the footstool. Then, I went to work on him with my mouth again, as it seemed he enjoyed it enough to allow himself to be so vulnerable.

Having him in this way—in a way that made him think it was he who was the master—it was a just matter of taking advantage of the moment when his head went back with his eyes closed. When this happened, I quickly removed the green cord I was using for a hair ribbon, which had been tied with a knot that the Algonquians used in rabbit snares, and drew his entire organ up in it, tugging as hard as possible. He exhaled deeply, gasping as his member and sack turned purple, looking down at me in disbelief. I held a long sharp hair pin to his most sensitive of skins, and made a *shh* sound, warning him to be quiet.

"Karten, Briefe, und Pläne, mein Herr Colonel," I said in perfect German, with a tug and jab for punctuation. The colonel could not believe how quickly his luck had turned, and still in my grip, minced in obvious pain over to a wall with a still-life painting hanging on it. While his cock and balls were turning a deeper violet and swelling, the rest of him was getting paler and seemingly deflated.

He motioned desperately to the painting, arms starting to flail and shake. I told him to flip the painting, which he tried to do, but it crashed to the ground. I knew that since there was no German who disliked beer, there was no soldier awake in Trenton, and no one would have heard the clamor. It was obvious the documents I wanted were stashed in a small portfolio, glued to the back of the painting.

I told him to remove the retaining paper, which he did until the plans, maps and correspondence fell out onto the floor. We then looked at one another, him down at me from above with a heavily pained expression, and me still on my knees savoring my Liberty. How different our roles as master and captive, though. He was barely upright, swooning from the aphrodisiac-laced liquor, intercourse, and pain. And I was crouched like a fierce and cunning forest huntress, about to take my prey.

"Achtung," I commanded, and he snapped to, at attention with a grimace for what was coming next. His cock, like a little soldier itself, was still at attention too, and with a single kiss to its head, it discharged all over the colonel's stomach. At such release, he fell to his knees, trying to maintain consciousness, but his attempts were in vain. He fainted, hitting his head against the fireplace.

I gathered up the portfolio of war documents, and placed them in a courier's satchel which I found. In the dressing room, I grabbed the rudiments of the Hessian uniform: breeches, overcoat, boots, hat, and a powdered wig. I furiously dressed, and as I was exiting the colonel's quarters, I slowly took stock of the night around me.

Thankfully, it snowed only lightly now. And yes, the ale brewed by Mr. Samuel Adams—with tincture of hemp added—had done its job. There were not even sentries awake or soldiers in the stables; the camp was dead in slumber. I had with certainty secured the Continental Army's element of surprise.

I stole a horse and made my way from the encampment to the direction of John's Ferry. The troops who were in an advance position from the main regiment were surprised to see a lone Hessian stripping off his hat and wig, yelling in a high English trill, "'Tis me, Penny Gooden-Plenny."

This identification had no effect as to their lowering their weapons. I regained my composure and declared General Washington's password for the surprise attack: "Victory or Death."

They took me away, threw me on the back of a horse with an unknown officer, and moved me to the back of the regiments. It had stopped snowing, but the ground was icy. Apparently, some rumor of my incapacitating the Hessians traveled among the troops faster than the officer's steed. It was incredibly moving to see the young Revolutionaries — some standing in snow stained with the blood of their feet because they had no boots and no protection against the elements — how they raised their muskets high overhead in silent cheer as we passed.

By noon the whole matter was over, and the captive Hessians and their supplies were en route to Pennsylvania. In the evening, General Greene himself informed me that the colonel had been mortally wounded in the melee. I felt nothing, except the thought did occur to me that while I had a hand in this man's death, he had played a great part in my many — as is said among the French — *petites morts*.

Your faithful servant, Penny Gooden-Plenny.

ABOUT THE AUTHORS

MINA VAUGHN

Kink with a Wink. Author of the DommeNation series. Mina Vaughn is an international woman of mystery and a shoe whore with a heart of gold. When she's not writing her unique brand of silly smut, she's plundering Sephora for any pin-up-girl makeup she can find. Mina's debut novel, an erotic comedy entitled *How to Discipline Your Vampire,* is about a punishment-seeking vampire who meets a quirky Domme with a serious role-play fetish, available now from Simon and Schuster's Pocket Star. *How to Reprimand Your Rock Star* releases summer 2014.

minavaughn.com

LINDA CUNNINGHAM

Linda Cunningham grew up a small town country girl and it is here where she's still most comfortable. She has written steadily throughout the years, although usually other peoples' speeches, articles, and grants, primarily for medical and agricultural trade journals. Now that her three children are grown, Linda is writing full time and writing the stuff she loves—Romance!

Linda lives in a romantic stone house in the Green Mountain State of Vermont, surrounded by her gardens and animals which include horses, dogs, cats, chickens, sheep, a parakeet, goldfish and the wild visitors who tiptoe through on a regular basis. When time permits, she also enjoys cooking, sketching, and painting.

www.lindawcunningham.com

JOY FULCHER

Joy is a fiery redhead who takes full advantage of the Australian lifestyle, sunning herself on tropical beaches and flirting with handsome lifeguards. She loves cats, books, and chocolate, and of course the male physique. Joy started writing as a teenager and never stopped, although she writes about much more mature topics now. You can often find Joy browsing the shelves of her local bookstore or researching her favorite city, New York, in preparation of fulfilling her lifelong dream to live there one day.

joyfulcherbooks.blogspot.com

KC HOLLY

KC is a single man who is a son, a brother, a doting uncle, as well as a corporate turnaround specialist, art lover, casual writer, avid reader, history buff, world traveler, cat owner, motorcycle rider, former soccer player, foodie, and wine enthusiast—a true man's man who fearlessly mixes plaids and stripes and understands the power of seduction and romance.

KIMBERLY JENSEN & SCOTT STARK

Psychopoetica, SPIN, Billboard, The Los Angeles Times, and *The Orange County Register* are only a few places Scott Stark's work has appeared. Stark's background in film and screenwriting is evident in his written dialog, though he's spent much of his adult life as a lyricist—a vocation that helps him bring dark, poetic twists to the fiction he writes.

Freelance writer Kimberly Jensen taught history at the college level before fleeing academic life to write fiction. Her work has been featured in *SELF, Glamour, Creative Living Magazine, Ultimate Motorcycling, The Los Angeles Times, The Orange County Register, The Ventura County Reporter,* and *Business Week.*

Both Scott and Kimberly reside in Los Angeles.

VIVIAN RIDER

"M'Lady's Secret Service" comes to us via Erik Ellis, who is the "curator" of the blog Comin' Up Holdin' Darts which leaks "implausible documents from unconvincing sources" of the type which Vivian Rider's grand-daughter released to him — salacious and slightly dangerous historical manuscripts discovered by prim and imperious bluestockings, students, and researchers who rummage through the library archives and farm sales of the last century.

cominupholdindarts.blogspot.com

TIFFANY REISZ

Tiffany Reisz is the author of the internationally bestselling and award-winning Original Sinners series for Mira Books (Harlequin/ Mills & Boon). Tiffany's books inhabit a sexy shadowy world where romance, erotica and literature meet and do immoral and possibly illegal things to each other. She describes her genre as "literary friction," a term she stole from her main character, who gets in trouble almost as often as the author herself.

She lives in Portland, Oregon. If she couldn't write, she would die.

www.tiffanyreisz.com

Young Adult Romance

The Ember series: *Ember & Iridescent* by Carol Oates
Breaking Point by Jess Bowen
Life, Liberty, and Pursuit by Susan Kaye Quinn
The Embrace series: *Embrace & Hold Tight* by Cherie Colyer
Destiny's Fire by Trisha Wolfe
The Reaper series: *Reaping Me Softly & UnReap My Heart* by Kate Evangelista
The Legendary Saga: *Legendary* by LH Nicole
Fatal by T.A. Brock
The Prometheus Order series: *Byronic* by Sandi Beth Jones

Paranormal Romance

The Light series: *Seers of Light, Whisper of Light & Circle of Light* by Jennifer DeLucy
The Hanaford Park series: *Eve of Samhain & Pleasures Untold* by Lisa Sanchez
Immortal Awakening by KC Randall
The Seraphim series: *Crushed Seraphim & Bittersweet Seraphim* by Debra Anastasia
The Guardian's Wild Child by Feather Stone
Grave Refrain by Sarah M. Glover
Divinity by Patricia Leever
Blood Vine series: *Blood Vine, Blood Entangled & Blood Reunited* by Amber Belldene
Divine Temptation by Nicki Elson
Love in the Time of the Dead by Tera Shanley

Romantic Suspense

Whirlwind by Robin DeJarnett
The CONduct series: *With Good Behavior, Bad Behavior & On Best Behavior*
by Jennifer Lane
Indivisible by Jessica McQuinn
Between the Lies by Alison Oburia
Blind Man's Bargain by Tracy Winegar

Erotic Romance

The Keyhole series: *Becoming sage* (book 1) by Kasi Alexander
The Keyhole series: *Saving sunni* (book 2) by Kasi & Reggie Alexander
The Winemaker's Dinner: *Appetizers & Entrée* by Dr. Ivan Rusilko & Everly Drummond
The Winemaker's Dinner: *Dessert* by Dr. Ivan Rusilko
Client N° 5 by Joy Fulcher

Anthologies

A Valentine Anthology including short stories by
Alice Clayton ("With a Double Oven"),
Jennifer DeLucy ("Magnus of Pfelt, Conquering Viking Lord"),
Nicki Elson ("I Don't Do Valentine's Day"),
Jessica McQuinn ("Better Than One Dead Rose and a Monkey Card"),
Victoria Michaels ("Home to Jackson"), and
Alison Oburia ("The Bridge")

Taking Liberties including an introduction by Tiffany Reisz and short stories by
Mina Vaughn ("John Hancock-Blocked"),
Linda Cunningham ("A Boston Marriage"),
Joy Fulcher ("Tea for Two"),
KC Holly ("The British Are Coming!"),
Kimberly Jensen & Scott Stark ("E. Pluribus Threesome"), and
Vivian Rider ("M'Lady's Secret Service")

Singles and Novellas

It's Only Kinky the First Time (A Keyhole series single) by Kasi Alexander
Learning the Ropes (A Keyhole series single) by Kasi & Reggie Alexander
The Winemaker's Dinner: RSVP by Dr. Ivan Rusilko
The Winemaker's Dinner: No Reservations by Everly Drummond
Big Guns by Jessica McQuinn
Concessions by Robin DeJarnett
Starstruck by Lisa Sanchez
New Flame by BJ Thornton
Shackled by Debra Anastasia
Swim Recruit by Jennifer Lane
Sway by Nicki Elson
Full Speed Ahead by Susan Kaye Quinn
The Second Sunrise by Hannah Downing
The Summer Prince by Carol Oates
Whatever it Takes by Sarah M. Glover
Clarity (A *Divinity* prequel single) by Patricia Leever
A Christmas Wish (A *Cocktails & Dreams* single) by Autumn Markus
Late Night with Andres by Debra Anastasia
Poughkeepsie (enhanced iPad app collector's edition) by Debra Anastasia